Till the
End of
Forever

I0641270

Till the End of *Forever*

VIVAKSH SINGH

Srishti
PUBLISHERS & DISTRIBUTORS

SRISHTI PUBLISHERS & DISTRIBUTORS
Registered Office: N-16, C.R. Park
New Delhi – 110 019
Corporate Office: 212A, Peacock Lane
Shahpur Jat, New Delhi – 110 049
editorial@srishtipublishers.com

First published by
Srishti Publishers & Distributors in 2018

Copyright © Vivaksh Singh, 2018

10 9 8 7 6 5 4 3 2 1

This is a work of fiction. The characters, places, organisations and events described in this book are either a work of the author's imagination or have been used fictitiously. Any resemblance to people, living or dead, places, events, communities or organisations is purely coincidental.

The author asserts the moral right to be identified as the author of this work.

All rights reserved. No part of this publication may be reproduced, stored in a retrieval system, or transmitted, in any form or by any means, electronic, mechanical, photocopying, recording or otherwise, without the prior written permission of the Publishers.

Printed at Repro Knowledgecast Limited, Thane

Dedicated to the person who saw this dream with me,
But couldn't see it getting accomplished.

The world misses you Papa.

Disclaimer

Many countries provide Indians with visa on arrival, but Venice isn't one of them. However, it has been written otherwise in the book and that is completely fictional.

A disease named Swasiomia has been mentioned in the book, which is fictional. And even if it does exist, then certainly not by the name attributed to it.

No line in this book is written with an intention of hurting anyone's religious sentiments and is there only because the plot demanded so.

Acknowledgement

I was 15 when I sketched this story. I wrote it when I was 17. It's getting published in my early twenties. So this journey is over half a decade long and many people have come and left in this while. This means, if I start mentioning everyone who has played a role, I'll end up writing an ambiguous monologue that you'll never read.

However, I would certainly not want to miss the honour of thanking the people who're my support system at the time I am writing this. A big thanks to –

Dr. Savita Arya, my mother, who also played my father and supported me beyond imaginable measures. The biggest chunk of credits goes to her.

Tushita Cial, without whose pressure this book would still have been a folder named BEBIAI in my laptop. She cast a spell, turning the soft copy into a hard one.

Satyapal Chandra, who mentored me during my initial days of writing. He still gets my back whenever I need.

Sudeep Nagarkar, who guides me selflessly. I am confident enough to fight all the obstacles in this journey as long as he's with me.

My publishers, for their trust in my creation. Lots of love and respect to Mr. Arup Bose for being so supportive.

You, who's the reason every writer is also a dreamer. I have spent countless sleepless nights imagining this book in your hands, and see, finally it's done. Thank you, *dost!*

Prologue

*S*ee.

Sometimes the writer of your destiny gets frightfully cruel, but you bear it all in a hope to reach beautiful moments. And after so painfully long, when the beautiful chapters are about to come, his ink dries.

But then, see.

That's when you'll have to serve your blood to let him complete your story. It might get painful, but the epilogue would always read – 'It was all worth the pain.'

This life lesson seemed to work for him. After so long, finally, he had something he could call a life. He sat on a bench, his legs dangling towards the beautiful lake, Jheel. Behind him the people of his town, Jagah, thronged the walkway – some strolling, children playing, others walking and eating from the vendors, all of them appreciating the calm, soothing, sparkling waters of Jheel. He, however, had something else on his mind. For him, those moments were like an oasis of serenity amidst a grievous desert, which his life was, before she entered and changed it completely.

He sensed something unusual as he contemplated. Just when he turned to see, a shot rang in the air. His blood froze at the searing sound of gunfire. Out in the thin air, from out of nowhere, flew bullets, one after another.

"Goli chali hai. Bhaago! Run! Run!"

The array of people fussed in no time. After a lot of hissing and hustling, it looked like it was going to turn into a lethal stampede.

Unknown of where the bullets came from, people scattered all over. His joints and his neck frozen, he turned his gaze towards her. She had pressed her trembling palms hard against her ears, closing her eyes as firmly as she could.

"Let's run or else they'd jostle us in the water. Come on!" he screamed, looking at the people running wildly.

"Where...are...they...both?" she stammered.

"They'd have escaped by now. Now let's get out of here."

They jumped over the barricade onto the walkway and ran barefoot, almost unaware of anything, making a getaway. He clutched her wrist with his right hand, and using his left one, he elbowed the people out of his way. His mind couldn't believe he was running for his life in Jagah, a place as tranquil as heaven. But before he could resolve the conflict of his thoughts, he felt an intense jerk. She had fallen down.

His heart sank in terror. Without turning back, he dragged her to a nook he deemed was safe to halt. And then he turned to look at her. He felt an intense pain at that moment; his senses went numb. Horror puffed his chest; every cell of his body strived hard to keep him normal.

She looked into his eyes with unnamed emotions. That look, he knew, was just the silence before the storm.

Faraway, his eyes sought the bench upon which he was sitting just a few moments ago. It was there that he had thought that things were finally sorted. But from now on, his life was going to be different. Closing his eyes, he braced for the drastic spin his journey was about to take. And when it did, Jagah would know. Venice would know. The world would know.

PART – I

"We're the souls broken. We're the hearts shattered. There is no face in this world that hasn't reeked of dry tears on the strokes of midnight."

"Let's get wrapped in each other's arms, gazing our universe, feeling the rain. Come, let's talk about pain…"

Livleen

*T*hose who decipher the enigmatic scripts end up encrypting their own lives. After all, there is no other way of solving the codes than living in them.*

Young Livleen often cursed his life for following the routine ritual of ass-kissing the rock hard chairs. He had to work for hours relentlessly because he was a high-in-demand ethical hacker and the only computer and networking expert of his town, Jagah.

Unlike his usual self, there were some moments when he developed an overactive imagination. Then he saw nothing else but codes and programs in his surroundings. Insects looked like binary codes. Housefly zero. Cockroach one. The hasty winds that brushed against his ears, singing the tone nature, seemed like waves of JavaScript code.

One night, an hour before midnight, he reached home and stood against its entrance. Arranging his dastar (the turban), he rang the bell. He was pretty sure there wasn't going to be any response. It happened quite often when he couldn't get ample time off his work. As usual, he took out the duplicate key from his bag. Making sure his head did not bump into the low door-frame, he led himself into the gloomy hall.

He jabbed at the switch. The dim golden light of the chandelier spread all over the hall. He was about to turn when he saw a glimpse that made him stand frozen where he was.

You've turned the lights on only to push yourself deeper into the gloom, a voice inside his head spoke.

His father, whom he loved so much, lay sprawled unconscious on the floor, the tip of his nose dipped in a pool of blood that gushed out of his mouth. He looked lifeless, even though he breathed eerily.

"Dad?" Livleen's shaky voice died midway.

"Dad!"

He ran towards him, knelt down near his head, and with unsteady hands, cupped his face.

"Wake up. Please wake up!" He put his pale face in his lap and reached out for his hands to rub them.

The house reeked of alcohol. As he rubbed his father's motionless hands, he imagined the events that must have happened. He imagined how his father Jobanpreet, being home alone, would have drunk in excess upstairs and how he would have frowned on finding his bottle emptied in no time. How he would have come running downstairs to get another bottle and how his wobbly legs would have given up midway.

Alcohol, my son, is such a sweetheart. It grows a new part of me in me, whom I can befriend. At least I don't have to be alone. At least it cannot see me alone. Alcohol, my son, is such a sweetheart.

The words of his father roved in his head and he felt worthless to even be called his son.

He took out his cellphone and dialled a number, struggling to keep his shuddering fingers steady.

"Hello! Hello?" said Livleen, wiping away his tears.

"Hey," greeted the voice from the other end.

"Make it to my home. Quick. Please!"

"What's wrong?"

"Quick. Please."

"Right now?"

"I need your car. Dad's not alright. We need to go to the hospital."

"Listen, don't panic. I'll be there in twenty minutes. And listen..."

If his shaky hands could grip the cell phone for a little longer, he would have heard the final words from the other end. But the cell phone fell on the floor and the battery jumped out.

He ran as promptly as he could in the somber moonless night. The grass was bathed with dew, making it burdensome for Ayaan to sprint over it. The continuous dashing had exhausted him dreadfully, making it difficult for him to keep breathing. But, he couldn't stop. After all, you couldn't stop when you're running for your life.

He gasped painfully with every inch he covered.

"Help!" his voice trailed off. The only responses he got were the howls of the hounds.

He ran aimlessly in the dark till his eyes shrunk to see something in the dark. His eyes widened within an instant.

He staggered and then skidded to a halt, thankfully just in the nick of time. A few more seconds of running and he would be falling to his death from about a hundred-metre high cliff.

Yet, as he stood gasping thus, he couldn't help but feel the irony of his situation. He had stopped to save himself from dying, but instead, he knew he would be facing death anyway. Just then, a six-foot-tall man strode towards him, a giant knife in one hand and a fire torch in another. A hood covered most of his face.

"Time has come to bid adieu to life, Mister Ayaan."

Ayaan's life flashed in front of his welled up eyes and he knew he had to die. In face of certain death, his mind began to explore the better options of achieving it. He could die by jumping off the cliff or getting stabbed in his chest or torn apart by the jackals in the bushes that only stood at bay because of the flame his attacker held in his hand.

It's better to choose a way before the way chooses you.

And then he heaved a huge breath, as if agreeing with the idea that had struck his mind. He took a step back to stand at the extremity of the menacing cliff.

"My knife wants to taste your blood and I don't like disappointing it," the man said harshly.

Ayaan's heart pounded. The jackals became the onlookers. And then, in the tense air, something happened that nobody wanted to witness at such a moment.

The electric power went off!

Frowns took over the euphoria on the old, wrinkled faces that were watching the best episode of their favourite once-in-a-week soap. Ayaan, who was sitting with a bunch of gray-haired people and watching his namesake character acting terrifically, was equally disappointed.

That's how every weekend at the Carlton Old Age Home ran. They would play *antakshari* in the morning, go for an outing in the day time, and watched television till late night. Three years ago when a shy guy had come to an old age home with a gang of orphan kids, people couldn't imagine how innovative one could get in selflessness. And since then, Ayaan had been giving the old people a new life. Sometimes they wondered if they could give him something more precious than blessings.

"He must have hurled soil in his attacker's eyes and then would have run from there!" Old Mr Joshi, who was thrown out of his own house because he had slapped his son who'd slapped his wife, made a guess.

"How lame is that guess, Joshi! He had his face covered with a hood if your ailing eyes could see it. I reckon he would have allowed the soil to fall down," Mr Naik mentioned.

"Did you just comment on my eyesight? My eyes are still as sharp as the gush of a blade. See," he pointed towards a sixty-seven-year-old lady sitting in the far corner of the television room. "From here, I can see the colours of the embroidered butterfly on Mrs Khanna's saree. It's yellow and red."

"It's a flower, not a butterfly," Mrs Khanna grinned. Everyone joined in for a laugh apart from the oldest man in them, Khan Saab. He was thinking something deeply.

"But what's the connection between letting the soil fall down and Ayaan's death?" Joseph asked with a broken voice.

"The wind would have directed the fall of the soil in one of the four directions. In whatever direction the soil would have fallen, he would have opted for that direction to die," he explained.

"The protagonist can't die. He has to escape," someone pointed out.

"I know!" Khan Saab interrupted. "I guess he would have thrown the soil on the fire torch of his attacker and extinguished it. That would have made it extremely comfortable for the jackals to come out and devour their prey. And when the jackals would have come out to attack, he would have jumped off the cliff and then, I guess, they would show him falling in a lake and he would survive and his attacker would die up there."

His guess made everyone think his way and in no time they all begun to clap for him. Ayaan even whistled for him. Mr Khan blushed.

By the time everyone was done with the guesses, Ayaan's phone came to life.

Livleen calling…

❖

Livleen rubbed Joban's plump chest. He could feel some movement in him. Motivated, he started rubbing it harder. The movement followed by a couple of loud coughs made a few broken teeth, along with blood, spring out of his mouth.

"Easy, easy!" Livleen looked into his eyes that were bloodshot. Livleen put his head lightly on the floor and ran into the kitchen for water.

Joban opened his mouth, letting the water go in. Most of it went directly in his mouth and a little fell on his beard and turban.

Joban pressed his palms against the floor and sat up, gasping.

Seeing his superhero struggling, Livleen was sobbing within. He remembered the time when he was a little kid and Joban would make him sit on his brawny shoulders and run around the house. He felt very insecure watching him lose against time.

He suffocated every time he discovered that his shoulders were too fragile to carry the burden of his father's feelings. Ever since his mother was abducted, when he was just six, he had tried his level best to be an ideal son and had failed all those times. At least that's what he thought.

"You're late today?" Joban spoke as if everything was normal.

"Why the hell do you drink so much? Do you know what I have to bear?" Livleen raised his voice.

"Yes, I know." He nodded. "I apologize; my drinking habit makes you bear a lot of my alcoholic farts." As usual, Joban found a way out to make the atmosphere amusing.

That's the kind of person he was. A Sikh, never sick of anything.

"Do you think it's funny?"

Joban came closer to him and patted his cheek. His anger evaporated as Joban did that. "Smile, son. If it's funny, smile. If it's not, smile for how funnily non-funny it is. Son, life will give you pain at every moment, but remember, all you have to do is smile."

Livleen lowered his gaze, sensing what Joban meant. "I know, Dad. But have you ever thought of what happens to me every time I see you sprawled on the floor, drunk?"

"Yes, I do. But even before I can reach any conclusion, I am on the ground again, drunk and sprawled." He guffawed so loud that it hurt his lungs.

"Shut up, Dad," Livleen giggled. "Ayaan's on his way. Get ready for some injections."

"I think no hospital can treat me better than a nap would. I am exhausted. Please?"

"Uh, alright. But make sure you take a shower before you sleep."

Livleen watched him disappear behind the walls of his room and thought of what life had tried to bring out of his father and what eventually had come out.

The doorbell rang.

"Where's he?" Ayaan stepped in.

"He's fine now. He said he needed a nap and I didn't force him."

"The same issue, again?" Ayaan asked.

"I don't know what I should do. Luv's coming back tomorrow for three days and if she sees him this way, it'll affect her studies."

"She's coming tomorrow?"

"Yeah. You'd come to pick her?"

"As she says, never say never."

Avani

The maroon curtains were wide open to give Avani the best view she could get from her train window. Her love for nature was lucid from the way her eyes swivelled as wide as the window frame allowed them to capture the whole scenic beauty. When her train whizzed over the river or in between the verdant alleys, euphoria struck her.

A silent girl has the most talkative conscience, and she was an indisputable example of it. Not that she hated to converse or liked to be left alone, but she had found no one whose words could comfort her more than her own. She'd learned to live a life within herself, or perhaps was forced into learning it.

Though she knew that all the ill feelings that swallowed her with every breath were just mere chimeras created by none other than her own brain, she could do nothing but surrender herself to it. Helplessness, though, was the worst kind of feeling one can have. It teases you by presenting all the solutions you could opt for escape, and just when you're about to pick one, it slashes your hands and all you can do is get tortured. But she was helpless to even get rid of helplessness.

Since so long, in a loop, her headphones played the same song, but every time some or the other line of the song would send her in a parallel world and she would return only when it was replayed.

Cupid, draw back your bow
And let your arrow go
Straight to my lover's heart for me, for me
Cupid please hear my cry
And let your arrow fly
Straight into my lover's heart for me...

Little Avani would ask her mom about what cupids did and *she* would sing her this song. Avani would ask if they really were real and her mom would twitch her tiny nose and nod. And since then, she believed in cupids. Whether they're real or not wasn't a topic of debate for her. Her mom said they were and that was what mattered. Cupids were real, just like clouds were made of cotton and babies were born out of sweet boxes. Not her mother, but her father said so, and Pa could never be wrong.

Apart from living life at its fullest, art was something she admired to her core. Art is a bridge between the world that you live in and the world that you want to live in, she believed. Be it music, linguistics, dancing or painting, everything took her in a new world.

At her left was her chubby best friend who had started cursing her for being so introvert on such long journeys. Unlike her friend Avani, she was clueless about how to talk to nature or live in art or feel the atmosphere. All she knew to entertain herself was to talk to her friend. But anyway, by the time she would have delivered a lecture to her about how to be an amazing co-passenger, their destination would have come. So instead of bashing her up with a typical Punjabi scolding, she shouted beyond the headphones, "We'll be getting down in fifteen minutes."

Disgusted with the shriek, Avani replied, "Calm down, Luv. The music is quite soft."

"Oh, sorry." Luvleen, affectionately addressed as Luv, clinched her tongue between her teeth and smiled. Avani shook her head with an even brighter smile in reply. The train soon whistled to a halt.

As soon as she stepped out of the train, a gust of aromatic breeze welcomed her. The platforms were clean and not so crowded.

"Jagah," Avani muttered what she read on the yellow destination board.

"Let's sit there on the bench till Livleen comes. You take the luggage. I'm coming in a minute." From her arched eyebrows, Avani signalled towards a bookstore kiosk. Luv nodded.

"How strange is it that by just reading few pages that are being bound together, you can completely know the person who wrote them? You can know about how he thinks, what he sees, and whatever he has learnt throughout his life." Her neighbour had told her when she was just five and wondered why people read such thick books instead of playing with Barbie dolls or sleeping on the grass. And she was enthralled after hearing that.

She bought a hardback paranormal thriller and caressed it as if it was a newly born baby. With a faint smile, she showed the book to Luv.

"Nice buy, eh," Luv appreciated unknowingly. She had no idea about the book Avani was holding or about any book other than the course books.

Avani put it in the bag once she was done smelling it.

"Does Livleen wear a dastar?" Avani asked.

"Yes. That's the only plump thing on his lean frame. But he looks cute. And you know when he smiles, he looks like a toddler." Luv grinned. Avani was still smiling.

"Here he is!" Luv ran towards a young boy with an azure turban on his head, a tender beard on his face and a loose tee shirt on his thin physique. Luv jumped on him and hugged him as tight as she could.

"Liv, my brother, I missed you so much." She kissed his cheek. He struggled to get free of her strong hold and breaths.

"I missed you even more," he said uncomfortably.

"And how come this stud took out time to come and see me?" Luv punched a boy who stood next to Livleen. He was tall and broad-shouldered, with a mop of dark trimmed hair and heavy, solemn brows that were offset by a shy grin.

"Livleen, she's Avani, the one I was talking about," Luvleen introduced them.

"She mentions you quite often. Welcome to Jagah." Livleen shook hands with her.

"Thank you." She nodded and smiled.

"And Avani, he's –"

"Luv," Livleen interrupted her midway. "Dad told me that Karanpreet bhai's train would pass through here in ten minutes. So let's go and meet him. His train wouldn't stop for more than a minute."

"Karanpreet bhai is passing through Jagah without visiting home?"

"He has a business meeting this evening in Kasba, so he can't. Platform number three, let's go!" he said.

"You look after the luggage. We'll be back in no time!" Luv shouted after she ran a few metres. They were gone before Avani could say something.

She felt scared there, alone with one of *their* friends she knew nothing about. That was the kind of girl Avani had become ever since her past had bashed her hard. She would be scared to find herself alone in crowded places.

"Hello." The boy offered a handshake. "I am Ayaan."

Her smile erupted. Her palms got sweaty and she could not look up at him. It was difficult for her to face new people.

"Avani." With a trailing smile on her face, she shook her shaky hands with him.

She looked here and there, at the pillars and at the sheds; anywhere but at him or anybody else.

"Can I ask you something?" Ayaan asked.

He was smiling and a dimple flashed from behind his faint stubble. "Umm... ah, yes," she stammered and looked away.

"Your eyes, their colour... they're brown or are they green?"

The smile returned. Not only the question but also the innocence of it was what made her a little comfortable. Nobody had asked her anything apart from coffee or why she cried in the corner of rooms.

"Neither brown nor green, they're hazel," she said looking at him. He nodded shyly.

"We're done. Let's go!" The siblings were back.

Ayaan drove the car on the wide roads of Jagah. Avani, who sat on the back seat, enjoyed the greenery. A flock of birds chirped outside the car window as if singing the songs to welcome her to their place.

"Play some music, dude," Luv suggested.

He stabbed some buttons on the car steering and every space of the car got filled by the soft and dulcet voice of a girl, which pulled Avani's attention instantly.

Cupid you're so stupid
Just look down at what you did

Cupid you're so stupid
Just have a gaze of the arrow you hit

"Ayaan, you're such a seventy's kid. Change the track. Let some beats flow in the air, dude," Luv suggested.

"What's wrong with this track?"

"That's *so* yesterday!"

He shook his head and changed the track. And in no time, they were at Livleen's home.

Livleen leaped down of the car and took the luggage out.

"See you all tomorrow," Ayaan said declining their offer of lunch and drove away.

Your eyes, their colour, they're brown or are they green she thought to herself and smiled.

"Smiling at what?" Luv asked.

"Who, me? The song, um! Who listens to such songs these days?" She grinned.

Ayaan

Ayaan drove his car over the flagstone driveway and took the car into the garage.

His family helper, who was watering the widespread hibiscus, waved his hand from the far end to welcome him. Before entering the house, Ayaan asked him, "I'm starving. Is lunch ready, kaka?"

"Yes, Saab. You please freshen up. As soon as I am done here, I'll place it on the table."

"Kaka, what's the name of your grandson, by the way?" Ayaan asked.

"Oh, my grandson? Well, his teachers call him Preetam. His parents call him Preet. And I call him Babu." He smiled unveiling his brown rotten teeth.

"You call him Babu? And I thought you had a habit of calling your grandson Saab." The old man's grin sealed in a wide smile. Ayaan patted his fragile shoulder.

When the survey was featured in the newspapers, just a year prior to his retirement, Superintendent of Police, Dr Nitindeep Anand (voluntarily retired at the age of forty-five), was found to be the richest S.P. of his state. And even after his retirement, he had wielded his sharp mind in the agricultural business that only added to his plentiful wealth. The mansion, which towered over Ayaan as if attempting to intimidate him, was testimony of his father's luxury.

He stepped into the entrance hall. To his left, behind crystal curtains, was his father watching a news channel. On either side of the television, the bravery and honesty medals, shields and trophies were rested in the shelves. In his twenty years of service, he was considered as one of the most strict and honest officers of the state.

As he took a leap forward to move upstairs to his room, he caught a glimpse of his Ma, who was hanging on the right wall of the hall, in a gilded frame, shielded by a glossy glass. That was where his Ma had rested since he was ten years old. He turned to his right and moved towards the photograph of his comely mother, who smiled mysteriously at him.

Just like she would have had held him for the first time in her hands, he pulled off the frame from the wall and held it. Both his thumbs rubbed over her smile tenderly and he went back to his childhood days.

Those moments flashed in front of his eyes as if they were very fresh. With a proud gleam on his face, the six-year-old Ayaan would go to his friends and brag about how comely and charismatic his mother was.

"My Ma is the most beautiful," he would say in his juvenile voice. "She's got very special bluish-brownish green eyes, you know?"

And every time his mother would hear this, she would kiss his cheeks and say, "Not bluish-brownish green, Ayaan. We call it hazel."

And every time, he would forget that word. *Hazel.*

Her slender nose and big eyes reminded him of the days when he would propose his Ma for marriage.

"You're so beautiful Ma. I will marry you," he would say with utter innocence.

"But Ma is already married." She would pull a disappointed face.

"Don't worry, we'll do that secretly. Dad wouldn't know about this." He would feel like a genius.

However, if everything everyone wants gets fulfilled, there would remain no difference between reality and dream. And he knew he had to accept the reality, because reality is not a choice.

He looked for a cloth to clean the dust over the frame and found a cotton cloth on the table behind him.

With the photo frame in his hands, as he turned back to pick up the cloth, his right leg bent at the knees, but lost his balance.

The photo frame fell on the floor and his head smashed into the glass. All of a sudden, a sharp piece of broken glass tore into his flesh, and thick crimson blood oozed out on the floor.

The sound reached his father, who was busy with the television. He swivelled his head back and his gaze penetrated the crystal curtains to give him a view of his son sprawled on the floor.

He saw a thick stream of blood flowing from above Ayaan's eyes, but he turned back to his television.

W hat would have happened to the phases of the moon if the earth was flat? And how would love feel like if there was no hate at all? Avani thought to herself as she walked up a small flight of stairs. She and her friends stood in front of a mahogany door. It was the first time Avani had come on vacation with her friends.

Luv pressed the bell. A shrill sound followed and soon the door opened with a creaking noise. Avani could see Joban on the other side. The man inside, she saw, was short and stout, with a semi-spherical stomach and chubby cheeks.

As soon as the door opened, Luv clung to her father.

"Daddy, I missed you so very much, you know." She snuggled into his chest.

"Aw, my daughter, is that the reason you called me once a week?" Joban patted her head and smirked.

Luv pulled herself back and stared at her father, faking the anger. "I was busy with my classes, Dad."

Puppy eyes!

Joban kissed her head, smiling.

"Ouch! Your beard stings, my young Punjabi boy," taunted Luv playfully, giving her father another tight embrace at the same time as Livleen entered, carrying the luggage.

"Now go in and wash your face and hair. They stink so badly," said Joban, winking at her. Luv gave him a grumpy smile and went in.

Joban then looked at Avani. Her immediate reaction was to bow out of respect. And then as she raised her head, she saw him nod, asking her to come in.

"Welcome, beti. I hope you'll enjoy the vacations with us," he said as he cupped her face and kissed her forehead. Joban's affectionate and fatherly touch made her feel as joyous as a peacock seeing one rain-bearing clouds.

"There's the way," said Joban, pointing towards a flight of stairs that led up to Luv's room. She nodded and proceeded upstairs.

Luv's room was a boxy one with brown walls and a window that never opened. She parked herself onto the cozy bed and staring at the ceiling, immersed herself in thoughts about her life. She lay thus until Luv came out of the washroom.

Luv wore a look on her face that bespoke a feeling of disgust. Avani felt annoyed about her friend pacing about so restlessly around the oval dining table, constantly mumbling under her breath. Once or twice, she caught the word 'careless'. It made her lips twitch a little.

"I mean, which father would welcome her daughter this way? That too when she has turned lean after eating the shitty food of the mess," said Luv, shrugging her shoulders.

Avani could not help but smile. She looked towards Livleen and Joban, both of whom wore shock on their faces. Neither of them, she saw, intended to comment on the weight she had gained each passing day.

"What could have I done if our cook didn't turn up today? She's become choosy these days," Joban lied.

"Or could it be framed this way that she came, stabbed the doorbell for almost millions of times, and when she realized that her master's snoring in the bed, she left," Livleen said. "I even woke you up when I was leaving for the station."

"Well, you can still drive to the town and bring some food from there." Joban raised his brows.

"Car? You serious? Forgot how badly you'd smashed the car into the poplar trees two nights ago?" Livleen frowned.

"That happened?" Joban pulled back his face. Livleen threw his hands in the air.

"I can," Avani interrupted with a gentle voice. "I can cook if you don't mind."

"You can cook?" Luv was shocked. Avani nodded.

"Well, that's that then," said Luv as she rose to lead Avani into the kitchen.

The kitchen aroma soon turned from musty to spicy. The appetizing smell of tadka made its way into everyone's nostrils and within an hour, food was ready on the table.

Joban dipped the chapatti in the daal. Avani looked at him every second, nervous. He put the piece into his mouth and she saw a look of contentment pass over his face.

"Damn, what could have been a better way of starting your vacations than serving this mouth-watering meal to us?" Joban said, chewing his morsel. Avani couldn't resist a grin. Seated around the wooden dining table, they all began their meal.

Joban coughed and signalled for some water.

"I told you not to drink that much," Livleen said, passing the glass of water to Joban.

"Dad?" Luv eyed Joban, hearing what Livleen said.

"Not only that, he even fell down last night. He's broken his teeth and nose," Livleen said. Avani's hand stopped him midway.

And before anyone could say anything further, the morsel that Joban was chewing tumbled out of his mouth and he felt as if he was choking on his breath.

"Hold on, dad!"

It was not Livleen or Luv who had shouted, it was Avani. She pushed back her chair and rushed to him, lightly punching him on his back.

"Breathe, breathe!" She rubbed his back.

She felt as if destiny had come to claim Joban as its own. Her breath got heavier and her palms began to sweat. "Avani?" Luv patted her shoulder. "Avani!"

"What?" She looked back at her.

"What are you doing?"

"He was choking. He couldn't breathe, Luv."

"When did that happen? He just coughed once. What's up with you?"

Completely flabbergasted from what Luv said, she looked at Joban. He chewed his piece of chapatti, looking at her in shock. Livleen looked surprised as well. Was everything that happened just a chimera or was her whole life a chimera?

Joban stood up and caressed her face affectionately. "What happened, beta?" She just shook her head in response, looking elsewhere.

"We're going to the doctor right now," Avani said.

"What?" All of them said in unison.

"Yes. He drank too much last night, right?' Avani said, to which Livleen nodded. "It may cause swasiomia. It's caused by over dosing of alcohol. The food pipe of the victim would shrink all of a sudden and he would choke to death. I've been taught about it."

Comprehension dawned on Luv's face. Avani could see that her friend had begun to remember what she had explained to her after Luv bunked those classes. Without waiting, Luv dialled a number and asked for a cab.

Avani, on the other hand, was still appalled at what was happening to her. Was it she who couldn't get over it or was it the bygone time that wasn't letting her get over it?

"He's almost fine. I don't think he is suffering from swasiomia, but his blood sample disturbs me. There's so much alcohol content in it. I suggest you admit him for a while," the doctor explained to Livleen.

"I'll complete the formalities." Livleen nodded and stood up to leave.

"What did the doctor say?" Luv asked, seeing Livleen making his way out.

"They're admitting him. Luv, you stay with Dad till I fill the forms and stuff. And Avani, I will call a cab for you. You just go home and rest till one of us joins you in the evening."

Avani resisted, but she couldn't fight against them. She was their guest and it was better to follow what they said.

And just before Livleen could book a cab, someone patted him from behind. He turned back to widen his eyes in shock. This was not how Ayaan looked a few hours ago when he'd left them home.

'Ayaan, what happened?' Livleen asked.

Ayaan explained to them how he had fallen from the stairs and how his brows had hit the edge of one. Luv asked if he was fine and he nodded. Ayaan asked why they were there and was told the reason.

"You're going back?" Livleen asked.

"Yes."

"Why don't you go back with him?" Livleen turned towards Avani. She felt scared to reply. Neither no nor yes came out of her mouth.

J udging too early and understanding too late are a couple of things we people are obsessed with.

That's what Avani felt after the drive with Ayaan. He wasn't like the kind of guy she would get scared of. He was shy and decent, the kind that's funny, confident, spunky, yet humble. Throughout the way, he grinned at her one-liners, which she believed weren't even worth a smirk. And what made her comfortable was that he wasn't putting any effort to do a lot of things that she never needed. Everything was hunky-dory until Ayaan started driving on a deserted road. Her brows started showing signs of a frown and soon the car halted in front of a building that looked half as old as time. The walls were cracking and the windows were broken. He stepped out of the car while she stayed seated.

"You can stay here and wait if you want or come in with me," Ayaan said. She preferred to give him an ambiguous smile in reply. He went inside. Once he was gone, every second passed like a drop of water falling from the edge of a height – one after another, slowly and teasingly. She waited in the car for almost fifteen minutes, but he didn't turn up. She didn't want to enter the building. But, she finally mustered some courage and stepped out of the car and went in.

After four steps, she came to a gate beyond which was a big alleyway. A few paces later, she stood in front of a big rectangular hall. On its perimeter were rooms, just like her hostel. The roof was open and the sun beamed on her scalp, its rays bringing warmth that made her feel a tad bit uncomfortable.

And while she looked around for Ayaan, she felt a hand on her waist. Her heart skipped a beat. She couldn't dare to look back.

She almost turned when the boy whose hand was on her screeched loudly as if he was ordering her to leave his territory. The sound scared her. She closed her eyes tight and ran a little to make some distance between her and him. And when she finally turned back, she stood still, shocked.

He was a little kid. His face looked shrunk and his gigantic head gave him a creepy look. His hands were lean and the part of his chest that she could see was burnt badly.

"Leave me alone!" he shouted. Before she could react, he went down on his knees and started to bang his head on the cemented floor. Her jaw dropped. All of a sudden, she saw an old woman running towards the kid, and before he could hurt himself, she took the little soul in her arms and hugged him.

The old woman instructed Avani to move into the room she came running from and like a scared child, Avani followed her instructions.

"Who are you?" Her thoughts broke when she saw the woman entering the room.

"I came here with Ayaan," she said unknowingly, her voice broken and scared.

"Ayaan baba!" The woman gave a gleeful smile.

"You're Ayaan baba's friend?" the woman asked. Avani nodded again.

Friend. Would she really call herself Ayaan's friend?

She patted Avani's shoulder. "Come with me."

"You're sure it's safe to go out? I mean the way that..."

"Don't worry. Behind me," the woman instructed.

She trod behind the old lady through a dingy corridor. Even though panic-stricken, she longed to solve the mystery of the place.

Every room bore the same colour as the other, as empty as the next one, filled with silence and sadness.

They took a left turn at the end of the corridor. Rows of chairs and steel tables lined the sides of the passageway. An awfully thin little girl sat on the last table, alone, with a bowl full of mashed potatoes.

She looked at the food with acute annoyance as if it was her foe.

Avani wondered if anything was wrong with her and looked at the old lady with questioning eyes.

"Just wait a moment!" signalled the lady with her palm. Her fingers on her lips, she suggested Avani be quiet as she, with baby steps, walked closer to the girl.

"Oh my god, Rashi hasn't devoured this delicious meal yet?"

The growl of the little girl at the word meal made Avani anxious.

"Hey, you foolish girl!" The lady looked at Avani. She was shocked!

"Didn't you tell this baby that this food makes people leaner than they are?" Avani raised her brows.

Potatoes make people lean? Was I supposed to tell her that? Am I a fool for not telling her that potatoes make people lean or for not knowing it?

Before she could move to speak further, the little girl dug her hand into the bowl and took its contents out in a handful. She ate everything in her fist and then licked whatever was stuck on her fingers. Avani stared in fright.

The lady moved away from the girl and signalled Avani to move quietly towards her.

"I am sorry for this, beti," the lady apologized. "She was an Anorexia patient. The people with this disorder would not—"

"Would not eat the food. They've intense desire to get leaner and hate eating food. They, at times, even frown and get angry if it's forced onto them. Right?" Avani said. It was all beginning to make sense now.

"You're a medical student?" the lady asked. Avani nodded.

"Don't tell me this is a mental asylum."

"I am afraid," coughed the lady. "But it's sort of what you're saying."

"Kids, they're kids right?" Avani gave the lady a confused look. "And kids are never kept in a mental asylum."

Before the old lady, Mrs Bhaskar – the caretaker of the children – could answer anything, they reached the central room and the sight shocked Avani. It was filled with kids of almost every age and none of them looked normal. A few seemed to be hallucinating, a few were having strange delusions, and the rest behaved bizarrely. She could see a boy dancing alone in the corner with a weird smile on his face, while a bunch of girls were yanking each other's hair. And in between those kids, she could see a tall guy standing and playing with them. She could see the joy in the kids' eyes on seeing him. He was Ayaan.

"Yes, you're right; kids shouldn't be kept in a mental asylum."

She looked deep into her eyes.

"But this isn't a mental asylum. This is a shelter home for such children. It's run by no government arms or politicians, but by people like us. These kids you're seeing are those who were abandoned by their own people."

"That boy you see?" Mrs Bhaskar signalled towards a tall boy who was scratching his head unknowingly. "His mother used to strike him with a whip while having intercourse with him on an altar as part of a satanic ritual."

Avani couldn't breathe on hearing that. "And this twelve-year-old soul who's sitting with his face to the wall is diagnosed with schizophrenia and also is a pyromaniac. He would set small fires in his yard but nothing huge until he burned down his own house, killing his little sister and grandmother. These are the kind of people nobody wants around.

"And every time such children would be discovered around the state in gutters or dustbins, they would be sent to the police station. The police would strive hard to get some shelter to take them, but no one would display the will. And that's when I decided to take care of them. But I couldn't have done it alone, not without the help of Ayaan baba." A tear rolled down her cheek.

"Now that's a long story about how we met and how he assists me to take care of these innocent souls and I'm not sure if Ayaan baba told you about it. But you can go in. Just maintain a distance from them."

Avani felt taken aback. To her shock, she did not know the cause of it.

When she moved in, Ayaan introduced her to the kids and she, with a broken smile, met each of them, played with them, and talked to them. Those were the moments when she understood what life actually meant.

The sun began to display signs of setting and it was time for them to leave for home. She sat in the car outside, but her mind still meandered inside. Neither of them talked, but the unspoken silence that passed between them spoke much. She didn't know why, but somewhere in her heart, she felt that they shared a deep bond.

A bond of pain.

T he morning rays broke through the glass window, waking her up. Her head hurt; Avani was up the whole night, waiting for either Luv or Livleen, but neither of them found time to spare. The day had begun with a sandy whiff.

As she sat up on the bed, she began to feel excited, though she didn't know why. And when her half-opened eyes saw the needles of the wall-clock, her eyes lit up as if something had dawned upon her. "Oh no, I'm late!" she cursed. She hurled off her blanket and raced to the washroom.

The previous evening, she had asked Ayaan if they could meet again the next day, just before he was to leave after dropping her. He had agreed and asked her to call him at eight in the morning. She was late!

She got ready and sent him a text to come. The previous day, after what it seemed to be a lifetime, her inner crisis had found a shelter of peace. She liked the way those moments moved with him – not one after another, but one with another.

He came dressed in a black polo shirt and faded blue pajamas. He looked sweet.

"Hello," he greeted her smoothly when she came running down the stairs.

26

She gave a gleeful smile. "I am sorry I am late."

"Completely fine." He blinked his eyes, tenderly.

"How's the eye?" She titled her head to look around the bandage.

"Not much pain now." He put his finger on the bandage.

"I think we should consult a doctor again. It's swelling."

"And I think we should go for a walk." He raised his brows.

"A walk?" she squinted. "Now?"

"I know it's late, but it's all breezy outside. Let's go walk on the hill behind the house," he suggested and left her confused once again.

She'd seen people going on coffee dates, for lunches, drives, and anything else, but a walk on a hill? He was certainly different from others.

"You sure about it?"

Smilingly, he shook his head, clutched her hand and they walked.

The wind was strong. The sun had hidden behind a swathe of dark clouds. Breathing in the fresh air, Avani looked about her. Livleen's house was situated in a picturesque area. Behind the house, small, green hills rose. They walked through the lane towards one of them.

When they reached its bottom, she asked him if he loved reading.

"I've read a lot." He helped her to walk over the slope. "But now I don't get time to read. I rather concentrate on making people read my stuff."

"Your stuff?" she asked.

"I am a freelance writer for assorted blogs and web portals."

"Nice job, eh!"

He grinned and pointed towards a group of monkeys. The baby monkey clung to her mother's stomach as she walked around the bushes. The young ones were busy jumping from one tree to another. Her immortal smile got wider.

"How are you so much into the things people have taken themselves away from?" she asked, walking up.

A squirrel ran over his foot, giving him tingles. "What if they weren't free?" he said and plucked a yellow flower from a shrub. He offered it to her and she accepted it blissfully. "That's what I think every morning. What if we had to pay to smile? What if it was to ache in the chest to talk nicely to people? What if every time you wanted to walk over the grass, you had to fill an application? And what if walking over the mountain was a sin?" He laughed. "And then when I think that the most beautiful things in the world are most vulnerable to explore, I find myself the luckiest to get a chance to spend time with this part of the world that is so bare that it's almost taken for granted."

She felt as if he had revealed a secret that was right in front of her eyes, but she couldn't see.

"Actually..." she brought her gaze from the clouds to him. "You're so right, Ayaan!"

They were about to reach the peak when she saw a beautiful peacock dancing, spreading joy all around.

"You've got the gift to look at life differently." She looked deep into his eyes.

"And let me tell you that I love the gift to my core."

Ayaan blushed.

Together they reached the grassy peak of the hill. Neither of them looked tired. As if nature had imbued them with a freshness that infused them with an unrivalled strength. They felt the cool wind and the fluffy clouds that flew just above their heads in the thin air. Faraway, their eyes rested upon a brook that ran beside the farms. Avani suggested that they sit on the wet grass. Ayaan obeyed without hesitation.

"Isn't it beautiful to take out time from your life, for your life?" He swiveled his gaze around the widespread area.

"It really is." Avani played with the grass. "That's why I came here with Luv for a three-day holiday."

A butterfly came and sat on her nose. She tried holding it, but it flew away. Ayaan smiled.

"I wish I knew why life cannot remain this cheerful, always." Her tone changed a little.

"It's always cheerful, Avani. It changes, never," he said and looked at her. "The life which gives you the moments to cry is the same life which gives you a chance to smile, which provides you with senses to feel the bliss around. The pain and the happiness are hidden in the corners of this very world. It's completely up to you to dig out what you want from either of them."

His words had the magic. It was the first time when someone had forced her to think about the things that she'd never thought of. She was discovering a new part of the world and she felt blessed to be with him. But she knew there was something in him, hidden in the deep corners.

"Why, Ayaan?" she asked in a mysterious tone. Her hazel eyes gazed right into his brown ones. "Why can't you feel the pain?" The bond of pain came into play.

"Because pain ain't gonna live till the end of forever. Because every breath is an illusion."

"How I wish I could understand you." Avani squinted.

"That's the misery that has prevailed since the inception of humanity. No person in this world has ever understood someone's words unless his own soul has repeated the same to him." Ayaan said in a breath.

Avani fell silent, as if waiting for her soul to respond to his words.

Ayaan asked her if Luv came home last night and she didn't respond. She was lost in her thoughts until Ayaan snapped his fingers in front of her eyes.

"Huh?"

"What are you thinking?" Ayaan asked with a smile.

"Oh, Luv?" She faked a grin. "No, she didn't. Pa got shifted to another hospital, so... maybe."

Ayaan nodded. "So let's go down?"

Her heart broke. Ayaan locked his fingers into hers and they started to move down.

"I wish god halts the time right here and we freeze in this very moment. It's so beautiful here," said Avani, curling her lips.

Ayaan nodded so sarcastically that she felt stupid for saying that. Defensively, she questioned. "Don't you want it to happen?"

"No," said Ayaan and waited for a pause. "It isn't like that. I was just amused at whom you're asking for it."

"Who else other than god can do that?" She was confused. And then, hesitatingly, she asked him if he didn't believe in god. He nodded in response.

"How can someone not believe in god, Ayaan?" If it was anyone but Ayaan, Avani wouldn't even have given a second thought. But there was depth in whatever Ayaan said and she couldn't just ignore him. "For sure there has to be a god. Even a mere thought of a world without god makes it feel so vacant."

"You'll know tomorrow," was all he said.

"Tomorrow?"

Ayaan could see the auditorium filling over its capacity on the dean's monitor. He sighed and looked himself in the mirror. He had put on a pair of dark denim jeans and a skin-fit white shirt that lay under a blue double-breasted blazer. He was soon going to address people in the auditorium with his talk on atheism, for which he was invited by the dean of the renowned science college of Jagah.

Because of his articles on web portals and newspapers, often against pseudo-feminism and religion, he had become quite famous. But today was different. He was going to take religion and theism head on. His excitement knew no bounds. He would stand in front of almost eight hundred people to speak on, 'Why God Does Not Exist!'

The previous day, he'd asked Avani to make it to the college and had given her a pass for the event. He expected her to be there, amongst others, to motivate him. And within a jiffy, his cell phone woke up to a beep.

I am here. In the second row. People here are discussing you and it feels so buoyant. You're quite famous, huh? Well, all the best. Come soon.

A shy smile made its way on his face. The stage beckoned him. He stepped onto it nervously, hesitating at first, and then, mustering enough courage, he moved forward. The anchor was already speaking into the microphone, introducing the dean. He looked around and saw Avani giving a thumbs up. He wished he could tell her what it meant to him.

"...So please welcome the only Jagahian member of TFA writer's association, the author, and the eloquent speaker, Mr. Ayaan Anand," declared the lady anchor.

"The very title given to my talk – 'Why God Does not Exist' is wrong. I am not here to disprove the existence of any god. You can never disprove something that has not even been proven in the first place. I am here to just make you question the authenticity, existence, dignity, virtue, necessity, roles, demands, commencements, etc., of things and beliefs. I don't want you to be an atheist, but a sceptic.

"Not just me, but people of soaring intellect like Mark Zuckerberg, Daniel Radcliff, Brad Pitt, Angelina Jolie, Stephen Hawkins, Javed Akhtar, Sir Salman Rushdie, John Abraham, Arundhati Roy, Farhan Akhtar, Rowan Atkinson, Albert Einstein, Bhagat Singh, Douglas Adams, among others, are and were atheists. Believing in god is a heritage that's been progressing with every offspring, but if someone refuses to inherit that, there has to be some reason. And that reason is what I am going to talk to you about.

"God *was* someone to whom everything that was not understandable in the universe could be attributed. When humans didn't know where light came from, how earth was made, why day and night brought different colours to the sky, why it thunders, why they could speak, why they were born or why death happened, they said it's because a daddy sitting behind the layers of sky wanted so to happen. But god *is* someone who was believed to be the creator of all the things that we could not understand. But when we knew these things were not created by someone but occurred because of explainable phenomena, we refused to let it go because we're too weak to realize there's nobody apart from us in this solar system.

"And when people realized everything can be explained but god, they came up with their own explanations of god, and today, those explanations are called scriptures, and their adaptations, mythologies. Mythology, according to the dictionary, is the study of myths or any book that consists of collective myths in the body of stories. The word itself explains they are nothing but stories that were taken too seriously. There are thousands of kids who believed Harry Potter is real, until they questioned his existence and understood he was nothing but a character of a book, like every god we have.

"The generation of thousands of years ago didn't know why things happened the way they did, so they believed what was written in those books by people. Let's take an example to understand this better. So, to explain why the inner side of the hands, mouth and vagina don't have hair and how the male and female pair of every animal came to existence, one of the oldest Upanishads, *Brhadaranyaku Upanishad* explained in 1:4: 2-6 that, Brahma's daughter Sarasvati said to herself, 'After begetting me from his own body, how could he copulate with me? I'll hide.' So she became a cow. But he became a bull and copulated with her. From their union, cattle was born. Then she became a mare, and he, a stallion; she became a female goat, and he, a male goat; she became a ewe, and he, a ram. In this way, he created every male and female pair that exists, down to the very ants. Then, using his hands, he produced fire from his mouth and from a vagina. And as a result, the inner side of the hands, the mouth and the vagina are without hair.

"Now this is one of the most irrational explanations you would find, but things like this are what make these mythologies a book that was well accepted by the people who demanded answers, and anything that came their way was accepted. For me, this is a serious case of molestation, or forced copulation. People say religion teaches morality, but what kind of morality is it? Morality comes from empathy, not from fear.

"The Bible says in Genesis Ch. No. 1 Verses No. 3 & 5, 'Light was created on the first day' but the Verses, 14 to 19 from the same chapter say, 'The cause of the light – stars and the sun, etc., was created on the fourth day.' From a day, these verses refer to the six days that the Bible claims the world was made in. Now, how can the cause of light be created on the fourth day if light itself was created on the first day? Similarly, in the 16th verse of the same chapter, it is said that god created two lights: the greater light, the sun to rule the day, and lesser light, the moon, to rule the night. I guess the god of Bible had no idea that the moon borrows light from the sun and doesn't have its own light. Also, according to the Bible, the earth is 6,000 years old. I am sure if dinosaurs were alive today, that fact must have given them cancer.

"Please, don't get hurt. Question! Question, like I am doing, and if you don't get answers, don't believe. Why believe when you can know?

"Question the pseudo intellectuals like Zakir Khan who manipulate you to believe human evolution never happened. I don't think anyone here believes that evolution never happened, and even if anyone does, I can give hundreds of reason why it happened. All I would say is, 96% of our genes are derived from that of apes. And tell me, if I give you a cake, made up of 96% shit and 4% chocolate, would you still eat it as a chocolate cake?

"It is said that you should never theorize before understanding the facts because you'd end up twisting facts to fit your theories.

That's what the defenders of every religion do. Just like Muslims claim that Allah had mentioned it 1400 years ago that the earth is expanding, but Surat An-Nāzi`āt 79:27-28 reads, 'Are you a more difficult creation or is the heaven? Allah constructed it. He raised its ceiling and proportioned it.' Due to these and other references in the Quran, it appears 51:47 is intended only to mean Allah 'expanded' the universe in terms of spreading it out, that this expansion is fixed, and not that it is continuously expanding.

"Please note, that I am not saying…"

DHRAAM!

A deafening sound cracked in, while Ayaan was still talking. A peon came rushing into the hall, his face red and drenched with sweat. Even before he could inform everyone about the religious hooligans that had invaded the premises with swords and guns, people hotfooted down the exit.

Ayaan jumped off the stage and clutched Avani from her wrist. She was clueless. He knew what was going to happen. Ayaan kicked the windowpane and the glass shattered. He jumped out and helped Avani follow him.

"What is all this?" Avani shivered in terror.

"You cunt!" shouted someone from the far end. "Get ready to witness the consequence of forcing Shiva to open his third eye!" Ayaan saw a gang of people rushing towards him. They were all dressed in saffron shirts and had black tilaks stretched on their foreheads.

Avani broke into sobs. She couldn't take it. "Ayaan! Ayaan! What's…." Her voice broke miserably.

Ayaan clutched her hand and rushed into the storeroom in the garden they were in and locked the door in the nick of time. His heart pounded in his chest and Avani had almost fainted.

Through the little hole in the door, he saw a Muslim group come through another gate. Some follower must have informed their leaders. It was the first time he was seeing the two religious groups doing something in unison.

"That's the only thing that can unite these religious extremists. Violence!" he muttered.

Two boys, one from the Muslim troop and the other one from the Hindu group banged the door. Ayaan's heart numbed, knowing that if they broke the door, they could land in fatal trouble.

"Why the hell don't you fucking speak now, coward?" he heard somebody saying.

Somebody kicked the door hard. Ayaan grunted. One more intense strike and the door would give away.

He started to lose all hope. He had almost sat down when he heard the screech of a loud siren. He heaved a sigh of relief and peeped through the hole again.

Once assured of their safety, he opened the door. The police escorted them to their van and drove them to the station and kept them there until it was safe for them to go home.

For Avani, though, the ordeal had been much more difficult. When death was that close, every string that held one's frame tight loosened. But it wasn't just the terror of death that had petrified her. Whatever it was, it made her wonder how she could get worried about such a thing in the near fatal condition.

It was said that bad news travels faster. It couldn't have been truer. The unfortunate incident got aired and when Luv and Livleen heard about it in the hospital, the disquiet chilled them to the bones. Instinct ruling her heart, Luv called up Avani. The first time, the call went unanswered. She then called up Ayaan. Even he did not pick up. She dialled Avani's number again; this time, someone picked up.

"Avani! Avani, are you people alright? Where is Ayaan?"

There was no response.

"Can you hear me? Where are you?" Her words came fast into the receiver. No response, still. The hush on the other end of the phone drove her crazy. Before she could get more nervous, she heard a voice.

"Hello?" the masculine voice spoke.

"Ayaan! Where are you? What are they saying on air?" she asked, her voice jittery.

"Calm down, Luv. We're fine," Ayaan assured her. "Avani is a little taken aback from what happened in the morning. She's disturbed."

"Where are you? And what happened, Ayaan?"

"We're at your place right now," Ayaan said. "I'll explain everything to you once you are here. I will go somewhere out of here. She needs some time away from Jagah, I guess."

37

He knew that despite the target being him, it was Avani who had become shell-shocked by the entire event.

A scorching streak of sunlight speared through the skylight as soon as the clouds above cleared. She squinted, finally making a move in her otherwise quiescent body. She heard Ayaan hang up on a call and saw him come towards her and tuck a strand of her hair behind her ear. Her eyes blinked.

"I know how you feel." Ayaan said, rubbing her back. "And believe me, it isn't empathy but spewing what it precisely feels inside me. But if I knew it would happen, do you think I would have gone there?"

Avani shook her head, slightly, still lost.

"I wonder what men can do to men for something that is nothing, but I guess it's better to forget it. And, in fact, I think we must go out."

Silence!

The fountains spewed water high into the air, the stream curving downward to create ripples all across the lake. Cold watery breeze kissed their faces when their boat passed through a fountain. To ease her out, Ayaan had brought her a few miles away from Jagah, to the lake Pichla. He had told her that the quietness of the lake always uplifted his mood.

Throughout the way, Avani had kept quiet. She was happy that Ayaan had not initiated a conversation. Even now, when their boat, with just the two of them, floated on the water, all she did was look at her reflection in the lake.

"Ayaan?"

"Yes?" It felt good to hear her.

"Why do you think I feel battered?" A thick darkness mystified her voice.

"The rampage, I know. I know it was lethal and that has disturbed you a lot. But the..."

"No you don't!" She burst her lungs out. Her yell shocked Ayaan. "You don't know Ayaan. You don't know. Do you think the swords in their hands, and the fire in their eyes was what terrorized me?"

He remained mum.

"It was a chimera, Ayaan, that split me into pieces. A chimera of you know what?" Her eyes were sharp, penetrating the restlessness of breaths. "Of losing you!" A smouldering drop of tear cascaded down her cheek.

"I am not afraid to die. Because when you die, you do so only once. But when those whom you love are about to be taken away from you, then you die every passing second."

The sun now hid behind the shade of the hills. The crimson glow spread around them. Twilight had come and it made the water look like lava.

Their boat drifted in the water. They came close to each other, feeling like one, and then, as a gust of wind struck them, they distanced themselves.

"I know that your points have soundness, and somewhere, no matter how much I try to run away from it, I think I believe everything you said there. Everything, I tell you. But Ayaan..." She paused for a deep breath. "Why did you have to attack them?"

Ayaan broke his silence, thickly. "Do you want to know why?" Hi cold tone confused her.

She nodded.

❖

The only phase of life where fantasy meets reality is childhood. When you are a kid, you don't know how to differentiate between the two of them. So you never know the absolute truth. It was the same with me. I still remember those times, those sweet sweet times. The kisses I received from my ma, the dreams of diving into rivers of chocolate, my dad hoisting me on his shoulders and walking…

But those were not the things that made me who I am today. It was that eerie moonless night.

My father was a triumphant police officer. A man of prestige. Strict but polite, with an illuminating personality. I would pull his moustache when he would make me sit on his lap.

And my mom, she was a firm believer in god. Not a day passed when I would not wake up to the smell of sandalwood or to the sound of sacred metallic bells and chants of mantras. The holy smoke would fill the room and my father, he was an agnostic, wouldn't mind that either. After all, he loved her so much.

You know what? I loved my ma so much that I once wanted to marry her as a child. Sometimes, I was jealous of my father, but even then, my childish impulse knew that I would fade him soon. She was a true beauty, I tell you.

It was a frosty night of January when my father received a phone call from one of his friends. He had been enjoying his glass of beer near the hearth, happy and content. I was sitting right in front of him and as he hung up. I could see his face turn red.

"Come with me," he had ordered me then. And even now I wonder why he had tugged me along that night.

He changed his attire, the khaki uniform, and ran towards the car. I followed him with my ten-year-old legs and we drove off. I could feel his wrath, but I did not dare to question him. After a long ride, he pushed the brake. I saw around and stared at where we had come. It was a jungle. He jumped out and slammed the door hard. I trudged behind him in fright.

He rushed into a ghostly cave. Water dripped from the roof; I saw stinky algae all around. The path turned a sharp bend from where we could see lights. As we moved closer to them, the caves opened, revealing a huge secret den. Big fire torches hung on the irregularly shaped walls and then, my eyes fell on something that left me painfully confused. I couldn't exactly understand it then. An old monk who was completely naked, his body and face covered with dark ash, and his long rope-like hair tied tightly in a big bun, stood for almost eight to ten women. And a woman, who was my mother, was on her knees, kissing his erect penis.

"Hallelujah! Hallelujah!" sang the other women to the top of their voices. She washed his genitals from the milk in a vessel.

"Hallelujah! Hallelujah!" They sang again, as she begun to drink that milk. My mind numbed drastically.

I heard a metallic sound beside me. Reloading of a gun! Everyone turned back to us and before my mother's bluish-brownish green eyes could meet mine for the last time, my father shot the bullet at her forehead.

Poomph!

The bullet pierced her head and blood flowed out of the hole it had made. Her magical eyes then closed forever.

It became dark all around. Deep silence weighed on them. The moon sang in lamentation and the sky couldn't hold its tears. It started to drizzle. The caretakers of the lake asked them to return to the littoral. Long and deep breaths followed the silence.

"They promise you the doors they made to heaven that they created, so that you, who're gullible, can live after death. They say god is most intelligent and then they, at the same time, manipulate him from the rituals. Wow!" The frustration spurted out of him. "I can't hate my father for this. Not because he was right or wrong. But yes, we're just strangers under one roof. No hatred, but no love either. That has what the thing people want me to respect has made my life."

She leaned forward and gave him a tight hug. They remained like that until the boat reached its journey's end. No words were shared, but the tell-tale of emotions ran high.

She was late for dinner and she was already exhausted. Mentally, more so. She just wanted to sleep. She entered the house and to her solace, she saw that Luv was already there. Before they sat for dinner, Luv enquired about everything that had happened in the morning. Avani narrated the whole thing to her. After it had ended, Luv asked her whether she was fine. Avani just nodded.

"Dad is fine now," Luv remarked. "Livleen will bring him home tomorrow."

"Well, that's amazing!"

"But, Avani," Luv continued, passing her the salad on the dinner table. "I think I must stay here for a while until I am assured of his well-being."

Avani sprinkled pepper over the salad. "Yes, you should. Even I was about to suggest that." She munched the chopped cucumber.

"I feel awful about this, yaar," her friend whimpered. "I couldn't be with you throughout the holidays and tomorrow when it's time to leave for college, I can't even join you."

"Woah! That's it." Avani said to calm her down. "Where did all this come from? And who says it's the last time I've come here?" She smiled and stood up to hug Luv.

They hugged. She closed her eyes and just then her memories started to churn in her mind – her hugging Ayaan, the words that betrayed his agony, the ripples of water in the lake, the mental images of the cave, his mother, his past. She shuddered.

"Avani? Are you alright?" Luv asked. The electricity went off just then and Avani pulled herself back.

"Yes, I am," she said, her voice faint. "Please put the dishes in the sink. I feel exhausted. I'll see you in the morning." She moved upstairs, leaving a cloud of suspicion around her friend.

The morning that followed turned out to be dull.

But it mattered to her not. Soon it would become day and she would leave Jagah for her hostel. Though she could have stayed there for as long as Luv was staying, she decided it wasn't the right time.

"Good morning sweetheart." She saw Luv entering. Avani stretched her limbs and wished her back.

"Get up and get ready. I've asked Ayaan to help you find a cab for Sheher."

"Sheher?"

"The closest airport is in Sheher, twenty miles from here. I thought travelling for hours in the train alone wouldn't go well with you, so I asked Ayaan to book you a flight. He's waiting downstairs," she notified. "I need to leave for the hospital, so I guess I'll see you in the hostel next."

She nodded, but in her heart, she knew the confusion that was taking root in her mind. She wondered whether to feel happy that Ayaan was dropping her or sad about leaving the place she had found her home in.

Avani climbed downstairs with her luggage in tow. Ayaan stood below and nodded at her.

"The cab is about to come," he said.

She bobbed her head in response. She placed her bags near the gate and came back to sit beside him.

"So, finally, you're happy seeing me going, eh?" Avani asked, avoiding eye contact.

From nowhere, his fingers cupped her chin. A thrilling sensation ran down her skin. She felt his eyes stare into hers. The feeling was like no other. She hadn't experienced it before.

A mouse dashed past the metallic plates and a plate fell on the floor with a clang, startling her back to reality.

"Time's running. I think we should leave," he said as he handed her the ticket. She took the envelope and they moved out.

Ayaan drove her to the main town and called the cab driver. She wished he could drive her till Sheher, but then, it would have been rather difficult to let him go from there. Did she not want to leave the place that had given tranquility to her conscience, or the person? She couldn't decide.

The driver arrived like the wind. Avani cursed him under her breath. She took her seat inside the car and looked at Ayaan, as if for the last time. An awkward silence danced around. No handshakes. No hugs. Everything happened in a mess. The windowpane closed; she couldn't smell his fragrance anymore. "Let's go!"

A drop of tear drifted down her cheek. Joban, Livleen, Jagah, and Ayaan – she didn't know how she'd strengthened the bond with them so quickly. She cursed herself for not seeing Joban for at least once after he got admitted. She wished she could share some words with Ayaan before leaving.

She stood in the queue to get into the airport and for the first time, she did not feel horrified to be left in a crowd alone. After a long wait, her turn came. She handed the envelope to the security officer and searched for her identity proof in her handbag.

"I'm sorry, ma'am, but I can't let you in," said the moustachioed man before she could find her ID card.

Avani gave him a confused look.

"Ma'am, your flight is scheduled for midnight, and it's not even noon yet." He slipped the ticket in the envelope and returned it.

"But sir—"

"Ma'am, I request you to stand out of the queue and consult the senior officer," the man requested. Her eyes welled up. She moved away. Why was Ayaan pushing me away since the morning if he'd booked a flight for the night?

It hurt her to the core. She tried calling Ayaan, but his number was switched off. Tears glistened on her cheeks and just when the new Avani was about to turn into the old sensitive over-thinker version of herself, someone tapped her on her shoulders. She turned back with contempt.

"You!"

"Somebody's sobbing already." He smiled, wiping her tears.

"Wait," she pulled herself back. "What are you doing here? And why did you book me a separate cab if you had to follow me?"

"How would it be a surprise then?"

"Booking a late night flight for someone and then sending them to the airport in the morning so that when they get pushed out of the queue and feel alone, you can come from behind and say, 'Hey, you're not alone.' That's what you call a surprise?" Avani hurled out her frustration.

"No," he smiled victoriously. "This is what I call a surprise."

He handed her a ticket. Anand Ayaan, read the passenger's name. She looked at the destination and her jaw dropped. She looked at Ayaan with shock and pulled out her ticket. And when her gaze met the destination on it, she went numb.

The destination on both the tickets read Venice.

*V*enice? Are you serious right now?

Isn't it a part of this world?

No, it isn't. It's heaven. But my point is - where from, all this?

You want to go to the hostel?

Oh, Ayaan. No!

Then let's go!

Visa?

Visa, for Venice, is on arrival.

And passport?

You'd forgotten your bag in my car. I found the passport in it. Here it is! See!

So you'd already planned it?

No, I hadn't.

Then?

The hype, you know. There is this conference in Venice about the Non-Abrahamic religions. And Hinduism is one amongst them. They'd mailed me about the chances that I had to be a part of it and discuss Hinduism amongst them. They'd said they would send me the tickets if I get selected. And guess what, the hype that these religious hooligans made against me was enough for them to make last minute amendments and invite me. So, I had my ticket last night, making it easy to book one for you too.

Again a talk against religion, Ayaan?

No no no. It's just discussing Hinduism in the conference where there would be hundreds like me.

Can I blush?

Only if it doesn't harm you.

Why all this for me? I mean why all the....

Life is not called first and last chance for nothing, girl. Come on, let's live it before we leave it. When pain doesn't have reasons to come to us, why should we have them to go to bliss? I've touched your soul. It was rough. You ask me why you? So that I can chisel the roughness off it. So that it can get smooth enough to let agony slip off it. I am sorry to touch it when it is rugged, without asking you. But, would you let me touch it again, when it gets healed?

How... how... how do you know?

I told you, I have touched it.

Their hotel was a huge one, built in an Italian Gothic style, with tombs on its head and cultural art engraved on the walls. The gate let them into a big reception hall, high and vaulted, featuring engraved angels on the inner curves of the tomb.

"*Ciao, Boungiorno! Benvegnùi,*" the receptionist greeted.

Ayaan stared him with a blank expression. Avani nodded awkwardly.

"You speak English?"

"Oh yeah, that's what we understand," Avani replied with relief.

"I see. I'm sorry." The short man apologized. "How may I help you?"

"Booking for Ayaan Anand?"

"Let me check, sir." He looked at his desktop for a while. "Sorry, sir, no rooms in this name."

"A-Y-A-A-N A-N-A-N-D from India. Would you please recheck?"

He scrutinized the screen with tense looks this time and shook his head. "No rooms, sir."

Ayaan's look of glee vanished off his face.

"Hey!" They heard someone rushing from behind. A tall man with not-so-formal looks ran towards them. His face was untrimmed and eyes bloodshot, as if he had just woken up from sleep. "You're from India? Mr Ayaan Anand?"

"Yes, I am Ayaan."

"I am sorry." He gasped for a while before speaking any further. "I am Joe Mardio, your attendant and companion for the VRD conference. I apologize I am late."

"It's okay, Mr J?"

"Joe Mardio!"

"Mr Joe Mardio. It wasn't so hard to reach here from the airport." Ayaan offered a handshake.

He shook hands with Ayaan. "Please check in, sir."

"They say I have no room booked here."

Joe looked at the receptionist and spoke something that was alien to Ayaan and Avani. "I am really sorry, sir, I forgot to—"

Joe's cell phone beeped and as he took it out of his pocket, his eyes turned watery. He slipped the cell phone back quickly, looked up at Ayaan, and smiled.

"I am in such a mess these days. I hope you don't mind if I book it for you now?"

"Can you please get us two rooms?" Ayaan requested Joe, signalling towards Avani. "I'll look after the expenses, don't worry."

"Not an issue," he said and got them two keys. "Mr Anand, I lost your contact number by mistake. May I have it again?" he asked and brought his cell phone to life to dial Ayaan's number.

"Yeah, sure. It's nine one ..." Before he could say any further, a call flashed on Joe's cell phone. Tension spread on his face again. He hung up the call and passed Ayaan an apologetic glance.

A caretaker took their luggage and they climbed the spiral staircase. The hotel was beautiful. "Room number 202 and 203."

"Thank you," Ayaan said and offered the man a tip.

Before opening the door, Ayaan looked into Avani's eyes, asking if she was happy.

She smiled.

Ayaan put his bags on the sofa and stared at the exotic room. A golden lamp light made the stories of the wall paintings demonstrable. A velvety carpet was laid over the marble floor. There was a window behind the bed from where the celestial canal could be seen. He took off his shoes and jumped on the bed.

The cottony feel of the bed gave him a sense of déjà vu. He tried hard to remember what it was. He could feel it. That room with the whiff of cloves, that smile on that pretty face, the sound of a lullaby in that soft voice. Memories penetrated his mind; he was taken back in time to the touch and feel of a familiar figure. He now lay in the lap of his mother, a mother with a mystical voice, a mother with the heart of cotton, a mother with a handful of life remaining, a mother with bluish-brownish green eyes.

Avani reminded him of that caring woman, his mother. Every time he would look into her eyes, he could feel time stopping.

"I am going to the temple. When Dad comes, let him know I would be late. Love you, Ayaan."

"Give me a kiss, Ma."

"Ma is running late, baba. You'll have plenty of kisses once I return. And do not forget to light a lamp in the eve. Remember, god loves you. Bye."

He closed his eyes.

Plenty of kisses when I return.

Someone knocked on the door. It was Avani.

"You haven't changed yet? The sun's already down and I've read that the boats do not run after quarter to ten," Avani said and sat on the bed.

"We're going somewhere?" Ayaan asked, looking at the canal below their room. The royal building was lit up with golden and silver lights.

"Miles far to sleep in a bed, huh?" She tilted her head and looked at him.

"You look beautiful when you look at people this way." Ayaan winked at her. Her cheeks reddened. Some people are great at hiding pain and some, at finding pain. Ayaan wasn't left untouched by either of these qualities.

Their boat drifted leisurely past the magically lit hotels and castles. They found the relaxed ambiance crisp, dew serving as the backdrop. Lying on Ayaan's lap, Avani saw the sky lanterns moving up, slowly, fearlessly, radiantly, and beautifully.

The mist pulled her back into the days of gloom. She wondered how she had breathed in those times, looking outside from her window, having no one but solitude to embrace her. Throughout those years of torment, she had learnt that there was only one thing that could heal the scars, a thing called time. And now, into the arms where she found solace, she found that sometimes time could be a six-foot-tall young boy with strapping, brown eyes and a dimple on his cheeks, with a heart that melted in different shapes of love.

Their water taxi hit the edge of a cemented alley. Avani looked up at Ayaan. His eyes were shut. He was sleeping like a toddler. How innocent he looked! She slipped out of his arms and whispered, "Time to sleep, Ayaan. Enough of those dreams."

It was as if he had heard her. His eyes opened gently like a lost puppy waking up from vivid dreams. He stared at his left. They were on the edge of the alley, ready to move into the restaurant for dinner. "Good morning," said Avani into his ears. He turned his face towards her like he was oblivious to the fact that they were together.

"I don't know when I fell asleep." He looked at her lips.

"You're tired, I guess."

They walked into an opulent restaurant. A buzz boy showed them their table and left with the order.

"Ayaan?"

"Yes?"

"I want to thank you."

"For what?"

"For making my life, life." She smiled.

"Would a piece of puzzle thank another one for giving it a meaning?" He poured some champagne into her goblet.

While Ayaan gulped his drink, Avani's eyes fixated at someone. Ayaan, sensing her confusion, followed her eyes to see Joe Mardio sitting at the table in the far corner. He looked restless. His cell phone was on the table and he was staring at it relentlessly, as if waiting for someone to pop out of it. His cell phone was in his hands and head on the table. She saw a stream of tears flowing down his cheeks.

A call brought Joe's cell phone to life and now he was talking to someone, uneasily, hurriedly. The call hung up in some time. He stood up and moved out of the restaurant in the blink of an eye.

"I'll ask him about it when he'll accompany me to the conference," Ayaan said. Avani nodded. The incandescent candle on their table kept staring at them until they moved out after the delicious meal.

Avani stared at the reflection of the moon in the water on their way back.

"You alright?" Ayaan asked, seeing her sitting numbly. The water knew what she was thinking.

She turned her face to him and almost shook her head. But... but she had to nod. How could she accept she wasn't fine? She couldn't lose. But she had lost.

"What happened?" Ayaan caressed her face.

"I can't hold this. I can't let it suffocate me anymore." Her words broke. From the very first day, she knew they shared a deep bond. A bond of pain. But never did she tell him about it. Every time she tried to unveil her scars, his touch would heal them. But that night, for no reason, she knew she couldn't hold it anymore.

"Hold what?"

"The pain."

Ever since I met you, I have come to know the deepest bond in life is not the bond of love. It's the bond of pain. I saw it in you. The pain. The world crumbles and the world resurrects, but what's immortal is pain. I have seen my world crumbling and I am seeing my world resurrected, but what's not changing in me is pain.

I wasn't this quiet always. Would you believe if I say I was a blacklisted student while at school? I know you wouldn't.

Remember the night when you spoke your heart out to me and all I did was hug you? No words of comfort, no promises of togetherness, no tears of agony, no glances of assurance, but just a hug. Because, maybe, when pain meets pain, the cure is in its embrace.

Why when someone says 'past', only the haunting memories flash against our eyes, I still don't know. And when I listen to this word, I fly back to that misty night.

I was all set to run from the hostel. I couldn't be there anymore. It suffocated me. I wanted freedom. That's the kind I was. I can recall the time when I shared my plan with a friend. Little did I know that she was so concerned about me breaking the rules that she telephoned my mother the very next moment! Had I known that, I would have never told her.

And unaware of the happenings that took place behind my back, when I got a call from my mother, I was shocked to know that she knew it all.

"No no. You don't have to do that. Neither do you have to suffocate there. Dad and I are coming right now to see you in the hostel. It would just take us an hour. You don't have to worry. Your parents are with you," she'd said.

My father, well, he was not a good-enough driver to drive the car on such nights, so I asked them to opt for the bus instead. And then, the rest is history.

The somber night. The mist that made other vehicles invisible. The water that the bus fell into after the accident. The body of my father, blue and swollen, identifiable only by the golden ring on his finger. My mother, pale and moist, dead in front of my eyes, leaving me alone in this brutish world. The promises that were left undone. The love that would never come again. Everything was snatched, everything, except the two dead bodies that weren't lasting for long either.

Your parents are with you, she'd said. She'd lied. She was a liar. A dead liar. A dead widow liar.

❖

The breathing became audible. It seemed like everything had gone still. He looked into her eyes. They were crying. Screaming. Weeping. Helpless. Alone.

"Tell me a way, Ayaan. Tell me how to escape," she pleaded. "Tell me how do you stay away from the agony that waits to devour you every moment? I know you are hurt. You know I am hurt. We know what we've felt. But why do I still feel it? And how do you not?"

A deep breath. Silence.

"What is an illusion?" Ayaan asked, his tone mysterious.

"Illusion? I don't understand you," she said, wiping the tears.

"What do you know about an illusion?"

"It's a kind of wrong perception for an instant. Like seeing a ball, just for an instant, on the floor where there is no ball."

"And how long is that instant?"

"A few seconds, maybe?" She was confused about what he was going on about.

"For how long have we humans been living on this earth?"

"What are you talking, Ayaan?"

"For how long have humans been living?"

"Since millions of years."

"And for how long are you going to live?"

"How would I know?"

"Approximately?"

"Fifty more years maybe."

"Isn't fifty in front of millions equal to the instant that we have in our life when we see that ball which actually is not there? And what do we get then? What is the existence of that ball? Nothing, right? No existence whatsoever. Isn't our life that ball? No existence before we were born and after we die, no existence, again. No pain. No words. Nothing! Existence-less. Isn't our life an illusion? An instant of few years against the life that's running since millions of years. Where would all our pain go? To null? Isn't it existence-less? We all are just instants, Avani. We exist for a time that is limited and then we vanish just like an illusion does. That's what our life is. An illusion of a few years in front of the existence of millions of years. Yes, Avani, every breath of ours is an illusion."

She stared at him.

"Just smile. Just jump in the air. Just feel the bliss and just taste some real life. Because it's all going to end. Because pain ain't gonna live till the end of forever. Because every breath is an illusion."

Winds gusted about again. She was trapped in his mind. The power of his words was working over her. Yes, yes, why am I bothering that much when every breath is an illusion?

It began to drizzle. Lost in herself, she felt his touch around her arms.

He looked at her. She looked at him. The pain began to leave their bodies. Their world started to melt. Underneath the milky sky, their lips touched for the first time.

Wrapped in the silky comforter, her chin on her knees, and hands binding the legs, she felt a tickling sensation on her lips. A beam of light barged in from the skylight and she squinted defensively, as if resisting the sun.

I never understood before
I never knew what love was for
My heart was broke, my head was sore
But now these feelings, oh they all are mine
Love burns brighter than sunshine

Her breathing became fast. Her lips curled up into a crescent for all the reasons she recalled at that moment. Her memories brought afresh the happenings of the night before. And for the first time in her life, past meant the flashback of beautiful moments.

...his eyes gazed into hers intensely when she stood up, reaching the height of his nose. It was drizzling and his eyes flickering. He smiled, making her feel comfortable.

He moved the strands of hair away from her face and while she was distracted by her fingers, his other hand touched the curve of her neck, making her lose her breath. She tilted her head, clasping his fingers in between her ear and shoulder. Shivers ran down her spine. She looked surrendered to him. He slowly started tracing the distance between his lips and hers. Her eyelids kissed each other. She could feel his breath; it smelt of the cure to her afflictions. She opened her eyes. He'd stopped right in front of her face, as if asking her to take the last step. She blinked and nodded.

Avani opened her eyes and now the sun was overshadowed by the thick clouds. The flirtatious rays stepped back. Her breath was pacing. She gazed through the window. The water was flowing like the stream of her emotions. Birds were singing the tone of romance in the air. The church bell rang in the distance. And above all, she could see the auditorium at the right, on the other side of the canal, where Ayaan was. She could imagine him addressing the people in a thick black coat, like a nerd.

Her eyes fell on the mirror that exposed her ruffled hair. The kohl was smudged around her eyes. There was a little cut on her upper lip. A earring was missing from the left ear. Her skin had some pink marks over her neck and bare shoulders. These were the signs, the love that she would never forget whenever she would see herself bare against the mirror.

Drenched completely, they walked into her room. It was filled with the mild smell of fruits. Ayaan sat on the edge of the bed, facing her. With some real slow steps, she ambled towards him. Gently, she stretched her hands to him. He held them and pulled her towards him.

Her arms were on his shoulders and their faces as close as peaks were to the clouds. He let himself back, lying on the bed, and she slept over him. He pulled a comforter over them, hiding her from the world, making her pain his, feeling the touch of ecstasy, giving away the heat that he'd saved through the blues, letting ardor slip into her, exploring the layers of secrets, tasting the lives within life, creating memories without words. The two warm bodies melted into one…

She took off her eyes from the mirror. It was time to leave the bed. She peeled away the comforter and went for a shower. A torrent of hot water struck her moist skin, letting Ayaan's aroma wash away.

❖

Avani had been waiting for Ayaan, but he wasn't back yet. It was almost evening and he had promised to be back before lunch. To add to her worries, he had left his cell phone in the room. She walked around the room relentlessly when she heard a knock on the door.

She opened it in haste. It wasn't Ayaan, but a caretaker. Avani couldn't resist the tension that climbed yet another stair. And when the man gave her a bulldog-chewing-a-wasp faced smile, it tensed her even more.

"Ma'am, Mr Anand has left a message for you. He would be late by an hour or two."

"When did he tell you this?"

"Right now, ma'am."

"Right now? He was here?"

"He was on the other side of the canal. He passed the message through a boatman and went away somewhere in a cab."

"Where?"

"I apologize, ma'am," he bowed. "I have no idea."

"Okay," she said faintly. "Thank you for letting me know."

The door shut. Anxiety made its way back into her heart. The needles of the clock moved like a snail. She trudged through the room in apprehension for two straight hours until she heard another knock.

Her hopes dashed when it was the same man instead of Ayaan.

"Yes?" she asked, hoping to receive another message from Ayaan.

"Would you like to have dinner, ma'am?" He grinned awfully.

Somebody give me a machete, please.

"Thanks," she faked a smile. "But no. I would order it once Mr Anand comes."

Slam!

She could feel something was fishy. She was all set to go down and enquire. But before she could, there was a knock on the door again.

The door opened and Ayaan stood in front of her. "Ayaan! Where the hell were you?" she groaned.

"I'll explain everything," he said and stepped into the room. "Can you please give me some water?" He looked bone-tired, his arms sweating. She offered him a glass of water. He drank three more.

Avani massaged his shoulders and asked if everything was alright.

He stayed quiet for a while and then responded saying that he was fine and there was nothing to worry about.

"You can take some rest and then tell me everything." She pushed him lightly onto the bed. "I hope everything went well at the conference." The haunting memories of Jagah flashed in front of her eyes.

"Everything about the conference was amazing," he said with eyes cemented over the ceiling.

Avani ruffled his hair affectionately and told him that she had been extremely worried about him. He apologized and said that he had something to tell her. He told her that he needed her help for the next day. Their last day in Venice.

There was without doubt something serious going on. She wanted him to sleep before discussing something that might tire him out. He closed his eyes.

Whatever the thing was, she felt assured that her new life had begun. Little did she know: journeys begin to end.

She'd spent the entire night watching Ayaan sleep, as if everything was alright, though inside she was worried. Ayaan came out after a shower. Unable to keep feeling anxious anymore, she asked him to tell her. He, without any hesitation, nodded.

"You remember seeing Joe Mardio tensed in that restaurant?" Ayaan asked, to which Avani nodded.

"We became really good friends in the conference. He is such a nice guy, I tell you." He rushed with words as she nodded.

"When I was talking on the stage, I noticed him worried about something, again. And when I was done with my talk, I walked up to him and asked if I could be of any help. He refused but I knew something was wrong. And, Avani, if you remember, ever since we first saw him, he would always get distraught whenever he would see his cell phone, right?" Avani nodded curiously.

"I wanted to know what he was worried about. So, when the conference paused for a break, I lied to him that I wanted to call you using his cell phone. Thankfully, I'd left mine in the hotel room. He handed me his cell phone and I went out to check what was wrong with him," Ayaan said and took some deep breaths. "I know I shouldn't have interfered and I didn't even know why I was doing all that. Well, maybe because I had really found a good friend in him and I wanted to know what was killing him. But whatever the thing was, I am happy with what I did."

"What are you talking about?" Avani asked. He coughed and said he'd found something in the message section of his cell phone that was really disturbing.

"There were messages shared between Joe and this girl named Kousar," Ayaan said.

'What messages?'

"The thing is that Kousar and Joe love each other like anything. They have been together since college. That's all I came to know from the initial reading. And when I saw him looking at me with suspicion, I hurriedly emailed all the remaining texts to myself and gave back his cell phone."

"Umm Hmmm…"

"And when I read them, I got to know that Joe would be killing Kousar, sooner or later."

"*What!*"

"And Kousar would be killing Joe at the same time," Ayaan said. "And maybe... maybe, I am the reason."

"A…A…Ayaan, what are you saying?" Her wrinkled forehead spoke the language of worry.

'The last day, the conference day, was the day when Kousar and Joe had decided to elope to Slovenia together. Actually, Kousar belongs to a conservative Muslim family and she was assured that Joe, as a Christian, would never get accepted by her family. So when her family was about to fix a meeting with their family friends to get Kousar engaged to their son, she asked him to take her away and they had made plans to elope. Everything was set until Joe asked her to postpone the plan for just one day. And that one day was because of me. He had mentioned about how I would struggle to get entry without him, how my dreams would shatter, and how flying away would turn into a nightmare.

"She had forced him but he kept on refusing. That was the reason they would get tensed about their plan and he would get restless at times."

Avani was flabbergasted. "And then?"

"And once he was ready to leave, she sent him a text saying that her family had fixed her engagement. She told him that she couldn't elope with him. The engagement was fixed for the next week, and till then, she was supposed to be locked in the house."

Avani looked at Ayaan in silence. "Why would they kill each other then?" she asked after a few moments passed.

Ayaan looked aside and said, "Because they can't live without each other. Joe's family pushed him out of his house the very day they got to know about Kousar, so he was alone. He has no one but her. And Kousar, well, she can't spend her life with someone she doesn't love when somewhere in the same world lives the guy she cannot live without.

"They've planned to kill each other the very day they get a chance. And maybe, maybe I..."

"No," Avani interrupted. "Don't blame yourself for something you never did. Instead, we should try and make Joe understand."

"No gain. We'd tell them and leave. And I am sure, after we leave, they would do what they set out to do."

"But we have to try."

"There are better things to try," Ayaan said.

"As in?" She inclined her head, peering at Ayaan.

"The things that I ran the whole day for."

Ayaan assured her that the plan would work. He had located Kousar's house from her cell phone's location and had personally gone into her house as a telephone checker and examined the situation. Avani was still unsure, but there was no other way left. It was still morning and they were done discussing the plan. They did not have enough time left to carry it out. It was their last day in Venice.

She gave him a soothing smile. He nodded.

"Listen," he said before she could leave to execute the plan.

She turned to look at him. He was right in front of her, towering over her. He blinked his eyes slowly as if asking her to feel him. Their eyes got closer. They basked in each others' embrace. Caressing her supple cheek, he lifted her chin, their noses almost touching. She closed her eyes and their lips met like magic.

"All the best," he said, parting the heavenly touch.

"Get ready, Kousar Mardio," she muttered.

It shows up in all promises
But happens, I guess, never
A myth on the layer of reality
It's a thing called forever.

Drenched in the warm flow of emotions, Kousar couldn't agree any more to this new radio jockey, Andrew Colton's definition of forever. Whenever she felt uneasy, she would dig her face into the pillow and listen to the stories on the radio. And that morning, when she was feeling as if her own life had ditched her, she could hear his words.

Had she known that postponing the plan for just a day would cost them that big, she would have never let it happen. But everything happened in the blink of an eye, more abruptly that she could have ever thought. She couldn't blame Joe. He was unaware of what her parents were planning.

She felt exhausted. She needed some rest. She'd spent a sleepless night. Her lids took over the weight of her agony, so much that they fell down, covering her eyes.

And when she woke up she saw a girl sitting on the chair beside her bed.

"Who are you?" Kousar's heart froze.

The girl leaned forward. "Easy, easy. Don't be afraid. I am Avani. Joe sent me here."

"Joe sent you here?" she squinted. "And how did you get in?"

"There was nobody at home. I just opened the door and got in."

"But everyone was here. Where would they go?"

"I don't know, dear. By the way, I have been living in the society next to this one for nine years. And Joe, well, he was my school friend. I just saw your family going somewhere together, so I hit the chance and came in."

She looked at Avani suspiciously.

"I don't think you're a Venetian. Plus, Joe never mentioned you."

"I am an Indian by origin. And I am not surprised he never talked about me. We were never so close until he called me to help."

"So, what did Joe send you here for?" she asked once she got a little comfortable. And as she was getting comfortable, Avani was getting uncomfortable. She had never done such a thing before.

"He wants to know if he can meet your family and ask for your hand?" Avani said.

"What!" Kousar exclaimed. Avani could see what she wanted to. It was working and now she was assured that the plan might work.

"And he is planning to come this evening to meet them. Do you—"

"Is he mad or what? No! I wonder what made him say so." She grew tensed. "Avani, you don't know my family. They are mean. They are very mean, I tell you." A tear rolled down her cheek.

"I remember saying to dad that I would marry a prince charming and he would nod. But as I grew up, I understood what it means to be born in a conservative family. I was forced to wear a veil in college, forced to stay at home for no reason during the festivals, beaten if I would forget to pray. Is this life?

"Is it all we are breathing for? To live with an instruction manual, huh? I know they would never approve. They would kill him, I know. They are devils. I can't live how I want to. I feel like a captive.

" A mother is a daughter's soul. I am sure your mother loves you like anything." Kousar rubbed the tears away and Avani stared on, as her words had hit a sensitive spot in her heart.

"But my mom, well, she loves to live a ruined life and she wants the same for me. This is the inheritance of affliction. For how long are we gonna live this way? Live? Sorry, let me correct. How long are we gonna die each day this way? I can't. Well, me and Joe have decided to die together. One death is better than millions of them every day." She stopped to look up at Avani with deeply sad eyes.

"You know what's more painful than having no family?" she asked. Avani couldn't answer. No family. This thing struck her hard.

"It's having a family that makes you wish that you had no family. You don't know what it is like to feel helplessness."

You don't know what it feels like to be helpless. Helpless.

She sobbed and carried on, as if in a trance, "They don't care about life, and the funny part is, I don't even know what they actually care about. I wonder what goes on in their mind, when seeing their daughter dead on the floor becomes easier than seeing her living happily with someone from another caste. I would be happy to die. Because I feel that would be the only time I would begin to live." Kousar couldn't speak any further. Her voice broke miserably.

The smoke that was rotting her lungs since ages had come out. She felt somewhat relaxed.

When she was crying with her chin dug into her chest, a hand came to rest on her shoulder. A touch of comfort.

She turned. It was not Avani. Avani was still seated on the chair. It was someone whose glimpse wrung the surprise out of her. Her mouth opened wide. It was someone she had never expected. The game had begun.

Three Hours Ago

"You'll be going to Kousar's place right now," he said in a downturn voice, avoiding eye contact.

"What!" Her eyes dilated.

"It is about lives, Avani." She closed her eyes; her breathing turned heavier. I can't do it. I can't do it. She had to defeat her fears to do this.

"I can do it." She nodded repeatedly her eyes still closed.

She opened her eyes. He was smiling. "Tell me what to do?"

"You tell me what would you do if one day you hear someone spitting out all the acid he had inside him against you?"

"Why do you have to be this mysterious always?"

"I wish I could help," Ayaan chuckled. "I mean, what if one day you see someone saying all the bad things about you that you know are true but never thought of? Like bashing you hard with everything he doesn't like about you and all you can do is hide behind the racks of books and listen?"

"I would end up crying, digging my face into those books, maybe?" She shrugged.

"Now let's assume it was your maternal uncle doing it. Your own family member. How would you react to that?' He squinted his left eye and tilted his head.

Maternal uncle. That was the last thing she would want to listen at any point of any day. Maternal uncle. Every time she would think of him, she would see dread roving around her.

I would go and stab him with a machete, she wanted to say. "What do you mean?" she asked.

"What when someone from your own family does that?"

"If he is close to me then that would be the time I'd have to bury my face in a book and cry."

"Well, in this case, I might do nothing different." He smiled.

"I think I know what you're hinting at, but please say it clearly," she said.

"You have to go to her place during the daytime. That's when she and her mom are alone at home. Just go and meet her mom when Kousar is in her room. She would ask you questions about who you are and what do you want. Just don't answer her. Just stay as mystical as you can be. Let her get confused. Try to scare her; not by any fraud, but by telling her the truth. Tell her about Joe and tell her about their love. Also, do tell her that this man, Aslam Javed, her fiancé, is a fraud who'd once cheated on you. She wouldn't believe it, but it would make an impact at the end. She might frown and get annoyed, but you need not get scared.

"If she asks you to leave, stand up to leave. She would stop you for sure. Because you are a mystery to her. A mystery that mentioned the imminent death of her daughter. She would want to know everything from you and you will tell her everything in a way as if you're doing her some great favour. I know it will be tough, but you'll have to be tougher.

"I cannot do it as effectively as you because women connect better with women. She'd ask you for some proof that would show the truth in your words and you'd tell her that not you but her own daughter would prove your words. Then instruct her to stay behind the door and listen to your conversation. And when you enter in Kousar's room, make sure you have your recorder on, in case she doesn't speak loud enough to be audible to her mother." Avani nodded, letting the plan sink in.

"Once you get in, make her comfortable. Make her feel that no one's around and she could think of you as her friend. Make her speak her heart out by any means. No matter how much you have to lie, just do. Make her speak against her family and make sure she speaks of their plan to commit suicide. All the harsh words she would say to her family might break her mother. She would start blaming herself. And that's when she would either call her husband to tell him everything, which isn't likely to happen, or she'd make her way in to share words with her daughter about where she went wrong; which, I guess, is likely to happen."

Avani was numb throughout. She stood quiescent, analyzing all that he said, imagining the scenes happening in her mind, thinking of everything that could make the whole plan a big mistake, wondering if she could ever execute it.

"Do you think I can do it?" She was already trembling.

"A few hours from now when I, you, Joe and Kousar would be exploring the streets of Venice to celebrate the best day of their life, I'd say – you did it girl. Well done!"

Kousar's place

It would be tough. But you will have to be tougher. She remembered his words the moment a thick streak of sweat glided beside her eyes. She crossed her fingers.

Things, on the other hand, weren't much different with Kousar. She felt as if she had stepped on a snake's tail, all set to be bitten. Her mother stood just beside her, gazing at her in a way she never did.

"Am… Amm… Ammi?" Her frozen words melted. Kousar felt betrayed. She looked at Avani shockingly.

"Look at me, Kousar," her mother said comfortingly.

"Ammi, I am sorry. I didn't mean it. I was just…" she couldn't bring up the words to justify herself. Of all the people in the world, she was the person Kousar wanted to confront.

"Don't be sorry." She shook her head, her eyes watery. "You feel you're our captive. You are tortured, right? Prisoner? That's what you feel about yourself?"

"No… no…" she couldn't help but break into sobs. She could see everything crumbling.

"Shhh!" She put a finger on Kousar's lips. "When you were just five months old, I had survived a fatal accident. I was almost dead, you know?" Her mother ruffled her hair. "And when I was back home after the treatment, I saw you sprawled on the floor. I had asked everyone why you were lying that way and nobody was even aware that you were on the floor. Neither your father nor you grandpa knew anything about you. A maid would just come and feed you every day. That's it. And you were just five months old.

"Baby, it's not like I haven't been noticing things in this house," she continued. "But I was quiet. Always! But now I won't keep mum. I can't see you so helpless. I am your mother, after all." Tears didn't stop flowing.

"Ammi," Kousar said, wiping her mother's tears.

Her mother lowered her eyes, swelled her chest with a deep breath, and with the blow of air, she said, "You're marrying Joe."

"Ammi!" Her eyes dilated. She peered at her with disbelief.

Ogni religione ha l'amore in esso. Ma l'amore non ha religione. (Every religion has love in it. But love has no religion.)

"Oh god, Ayaan, it's an airport."

"It isn't illegal here."

"Doge's Palace, Grand Canal, St. Mark's Square, Cannaregio, Venice Lagoon and Ca' Rezzonico. After exploring all these romantic places, you think this is the best place to kiss?"

"Joe and Kousar were with us, then."

"But they were kissing everywhere."

"What's so romantic about kissing a girl where everyone's already doing the same thing?"

"This world is such a bad place for such good kisses."

Ayaan leaned his face close to hers. "But this world is the only place where my lips can meet yours."

His lips brushed hers. She forgot to breathe.

"You don't have to be so sad. I've promised Joe we'd go there again."

Avani huffed. How badly she wanted the flight to turn back. "If it was impossible to break promises, Mr Anand," Avani said, looking out at the clouds, "promises would cease to exist."

"Ahaan?"

"But yeah, they still exist. So you know what I mean." She smirked.

"Do I look like a promise-breaker?"

"Then make a promise that you'll never break a promise." She winked at him. "Darn! That rhymed!"

"Is it a kind of a paradoxical trap or what?" He shrugged.

"Would you mind getting trapped by me, anyway?"

"How does getting trapped make any difference to a captive?" He moved his head lightly. "Anyway?"

Amid the thin air, hundreds of feet above the ground, smiles broke on their faces.

His hands wrapped around her body. She didn't move an inch, even breathed calmly so that he did not feel the need to take them off. She loved his touch.

The flight was about to land in India. Ayaan gazed at her. She had fallen asleep in his cozy arms, drooling unknowingly. He tried not to make any movements but still managed to caress her cheeks slowly with his fingers. The same fingers that were about to drench in thick maroon blood.

Back from Venice, Ayaan couldn't deny that there was something in the whiff of Indian soil that drove him crazy. Traffic jams. Road rages. Damaged streets. Abandoned animals blocking the path. On any other day, they would have made him feel like he was home. But now, it frustrated him. A monotonous journey later, they were back. Avani stabbed the bell of the gabled front house. Someone pulled open the door.

"*Avani!*" Luv shouted. "You're back from the hostel?"

"You aren't happy seeing me back?" Avani chuckled and moved in, followed by Ayaan.

"I would be happier if you say our vacations were extended for whatever reason."

"Even if they were, I am sure she's unaware. She hasn't even gone back to the hostel yet," said Ayaan.

"Where were you all these days then?" Luv asked as she closed the door.

"Ayaan took me to Venice with him." She sat on the sofa in the hall. Ayaan went into the kitchen for some water.

"What! You're high?" Avani handed her the tickets and Luv couldn't blink her eyes.

"Tell me you guys are kidding!"

"We're serious, sweetheart."

"No, no, please tell me it's a joke."

"It isn't. He was invited there for a conference and—"

"No. Come on. It's a joke. Haha! See, you got me laughing now. End of the joke, right?"

"You're reacting as if we are here with hands soaked in blood, asking you to give us shelter from the police," Ayaan said from the kitchen.

"Umm… maybe yeah." Luv shrugged. "But that means you people went to the mecca of romance, Venice, all alone. And I was here, uninformed about it. Oh, Waheguru, this mean world."

"You had to look after your father, I guess," Ayaan said. "Anyway, how's he?"

"He is back home, sleeping upstairs. Now tell me everything. Tell me how this happened and just tell me everything you would've wanted to know if I were in your place."

"How about saying it all after we're done with a much-needed nap?" Avani asked.

"Only if you promise we'll all go out somewhere this evening when Livleen returns from work." She looked at them with anticipation.

"There's no saying no to that." Ayaan winked.

Avani looked at him. He looked at her.

I love you.

I love you even more.

"And then Joe and Kousar said they would name their kids after us." All of them burst into laughter. It was drizzling, though faint enough to not drench them.

Gazing at the endless beauty of Jheel, they narrated everything Livleen and Luv were curious to know about.

"Why's it so crowded today? Anything special?" Luv asked, looking at the walkway that was awfully full of people.

"The weather maybe," Livleen said, "but anyway, we can't blame the rush when we are contributing to it."

Ayaan took off his shoes to let his feet dip in the nippy waters.

"Why don't you go and bring us some ice-creams, Liv?" Luv pointed at an ice-cream kiosk. "A black currant for me."

"A strawberry for me," Ayaan said.

"I can't bring four ice-creams alone."

"I'll join you," Avani said. They went to the kiosk, making their way into the rush.

Ayaan looked at the horizon as he swung his legs in the water. After so many years, finally, everything was sorted.

"Ayaan?" Luv said. He broke out of his trance and looked at her.

"Yes?"

"If you don't mind, can I ask you something?" She let her legs dip in the water.

"Go on." Ayaan nodded his head.

"Do you love Avani?" She avoided eye contact, leaving Ayaan confused.

He looked away, not knowing how to answer her. He turned his head back towards the walkway to distract himself. But before he could think of any answer to her question, from nowhere the sound of firing made every bone in his frame tremble. Someone had fired a bullet, making the array of hundreds of people diffuse in no time.

A lethal stampede erupted on the walkway. He looked at Luv, who was quivering badly. Her hands were pressed hard against her ears. The arena was dinned with the screeches of people who were rushing around awfully, with fear of death in their eyes.

At the far end, he caught a glimpse of Avani and Livleen running for the exit.

"Let's run or else they'd jostle us in the water. Come on!"

She couldn't react. His shriek was for no reason. He turned back to see people going mad over finding mobility. So mad that they cared least if they were dashing over land or over helplessly fallen people.

"Where are they both?" He heard her asking. He assured her that Livleen and Avani would have escaped. He clutched her hand and they jumped on the walkway. Nobody knew who had his grip on the trigger and whether the bullet actually had hit any skin or was it just a fire into the air. All they intended to do was to get out of the place.

From his right hand he clenched Luv's hand, and from the left, he elbowed the people who were being obstacles. His muscles had begun to ache but coming to a halt in that fatal stampede was the last thing he wanted. The exit wasn't too far.

Suddenly he felt an intense jerk on his right hand. The same hand from which he'd held Luv. She had fallen down. His heart froze.

Before turning back he pulled her to the side to save her from being overstepped. And just as he turned back to check on her, his breathing stopped.

He couldn't believe his eyes. A sharp knife had cut Luv's throat dreadfully. Her throat was slit, blood streaming out to mix in the water.

The knife had cut her windpipe. She wasn't breathing. She was dead. She had been murdered.

It was pitch dark. No movement. Air felt heavy on his chest. And then, suddenly, a beeping sound attacked the room. His ears pricked up, his nose could sniff medicines, but his eyes, they wouldn't open, no matter how much he tried.

He tried, but failed. He scratched the dusty walls, gasping helplessly. Relentless drops of thick sweat trickled down his face. Either open up or else get closed forever. Please.

He gathered all the strength he could. His forehead creased but his eyes remained sealed. He felt a sudden thrust on his body. Where? Why? And as his chest got thrust for yet another time, the remnant unconsciousness kick-opened the doors of his eyes to find the way out. He shot up in the bed, gasping awfully in a position he was neither lying nor sitting in.

Someone thrust his chest again. He gasped loudly and shot up in the bed. His eyes had opened again.

Everything he could see was blurred. A stained green curtain waved at him.

Joban had been unconscious for three hours. Now that he was up, he looked around to find something that seemed to be lost. Forever. His bloodshot eyes aimlessly quaked at the people standing beside him. His son Livleen was standing beside a team of doctors, and behind them was Ayaan.

He tried to sit, but he had no strength left in him. Livleen supported his back so that he could sit comfortably. Everything felt as if it were a nightmare, a delusion. His daughter was dead. And no matter how many times he brushed this thought aside, he knew he would still have to see his baby girl lying helplessly in between the pile of wood where her skin would shrink until it would be gone.

"Bring her back," Joban pleaded to Livleen. "There has to be a way."

Dad! Why the hell everyone calls me fat here?

I never called you that. It's just Livleen who does.

Why don't you rebuke him for that, then?

I can't rebuke him for what I taught him since he was a child.

You taught him to call me fat?

No, never. I just taught him to never be afraid to speak the truth.

Dad! One day you'd have to buy new dresses for me. I tell you, these are getting loose.

Impossible!

Nothing is impossible, young man.

Livleen closed his eyes tight and the never-ending stream of tears flowed down his cheeks. His hands still had the smell of black currant. Her last wish.

A police inspector made his way in with Avani. Her eyes were swollen.

Joban looked at the tall inspector with pain in his eyes.

"I am sorry for everything that has happened with you." The police inspector commiserated him. "But can you please come with us to the morgue to see your daughter before we begin with the post-mortem?"

He felt a twinge in his heart and was carried on a wheelchair to the morgue. It was dark, reeking of the foul smell of dead bodies. They walked past an array of beds. The inspector stopped against one of them. Joban just sat numbly in his chair. As the inspector yanked the cloth from over the body, Livleen broke down.

Joban looked at Luv's pale blue face. His tears dried into his eyes. He sat quietly, numbly, without any expression. His eyes stared at her.

He pushed his feet against the floor; he could barely manage to stand up. He leaned towards her face and gave a peck on her forehead. It felt moist to his dry lips. He turned back towards the exit and never looked back again.

"Sir, do you suspect someone?" The inspector approached from behind. He cared least to turn. "Sir?"

Joban came to an abrupt halt. He turned again to see him, his eyes betraying the flames of unspoken words. *"I want to know who it was and why he did this. Understand?"*

The inspector nodded.

He moved into the corridor and Livleen and Ayaan followed him. On the wall hung a television that Joban didn't pay heed to until it said something that made him stop and look at it.

News from Jagah. A young girl was brutally murdered in the town today. Police says the attackers had pierced her throat using a knife. This happened on the crowded walkway near the Jheel. The reports say that the murder of the girl was a consequence of the failed attempt to murder his partner. For further information, we have the SP, Mr Singh, with us.

"Sir, why do you think the attackers wanted to kill the guy she was with?"

"Ma'am, first of all, through your channel I would want to announce that we are clear about the case. The investigation says that it was an attempt to kill Mr Ayaan Anand, the boy who was with her at that time. The culprit provoked a stampede by firing into the air and when everyone was busy running, he used the throwing knife. He didn't want a bullet to enter in his target's flesh. That would have given us a clue about him. But his calculations to assassinate Ayaan went slightly wrong and took the shape of murder. And the girl who was just behind him got sliced by the knife."

"But, sir, why would someone want to kill him?"

"If you remember, he is the same gentleman who had badly criticized religion and god a few days back. Reports say that it was because of the anger he provoked in believers."

"Okay sir, thanks for keeping us updated. You stay tuned with us. We'll be back after a break."

The winds stopped. Ayaan looked at Joban. And when Joban stared back at him, his eyes wanted him to burn by its flames.

Joban's car raced on the irritably packed roads. The group of kids couldn't have seen the next rays of the sun had he not given a sharp spin to the steering wheel. His eyes were bloodshot. People started to yell at him, abusing, pelting stones at his car, and running to save themselves. But all that went unnoticed.

What perturbed Ayaan, Livleen, and Avani, who were following his car, was not only the pace with which Joban was driving, but also the bottle of vodka he had in his hand. Deep in his heart, Livleen knew Ayaan wasn't to be blamed for her death. But what could he do?

"Ayaan, please, you go slowly," Avani said tensely from the back seat of the car.

Ayaan almost ignored her words or probably never heard them in the first place. He was lost in his own thoughts. And when Livleen looked at him, he could sense the punishment he was giving to himself.

"Keep calm, Ayaan. We have to deal with it," Livleen said. Ayaan looked at him. Livleen wasn't crying. He was trying to make him believe that things were going to be fine. His gestures boosted Ayaan with something he needed desperately.

He kept following Joban until his car came to a halt outside his house. The father jumped out and slammed the door hard. He held the vodka bottle in one hand, and with the other one, he supported his body against the walls.

Joban gulped another sip of Vodka, and trod towards the door. His head was spinning awfully, but he didn't stop. He pushed the door open and he could feel the silence in the house. That eerie silence.

He walked towards the end wall on which Luv had made a doodle. A fat man, a thin boy, and a girl were standing in a garden underneath which, in a juvenile handwriting, was written 'I love my family.'

As his fragile fingers touched the little girl on the wall – her hair tied on either side of her head and an awkward smile on her face – he closed his eyes tight, pushing the bottle hard into his mouth. He heard a few footsteps approach him from behind. He turned to see the three children standing on the threshold. He looked at Ayaan and that exasperated him. Ayaan advanced towards him.

"Stop right there!" Joban breathed his lungs out. Avani and Livleen trembled from his shriek. Livleen didn't even remember the last time he had heard Joban saying something so loud. Joban turned back to move into his room.

"Dad!" Livleen called him from behind.

"No!" Ayaan put his hand on his shoulder. "Let me."

Livleen nodded. Ayaan walked past the hall into Joban's room with small steps. He saw Joban shoving out the clothes from his cupboard.

He walked towards him as if he had all the time in the world, making sure that Joban didn't lose his calm over seeing him walk in. He was sure about how to deal with this thing, but he wasn't sure about how Joban was going to deal with it.

"Why are you doing this?"

Joban ignored him, busy packing his bags. And this relieved Ayaan slightly. At least Joban hadn't exploded on him. Ayaan took a deep breath and moved closer to him, keeping his eyes cemented over Joban's movements.

"Please?" Ayaan placed his hand on Joban's shoulder but even before he could speak any further, Joban turned and kicked him vigorously in his groin, making him fall on the glass table on his back. The table crushed into pieces and the shards pierced him on his arms and legs.

"Don't you dare touch me, you bloody bastard!" He breathed heavily, loud enough to scare Ayaan.

Livleen sprinted into the room, followed by Avani who stared at Ayaan with shocked eyes.

"Ayaan!" Avani tried reaching him, but Livleen clutched her arm.

"Don't be stupid. There's glass there!"

Her face was drenched with tears. "Leave me..."

"What have you done?" Livleen asked Joban with a hint of annoyance in his voice. Joban kept his harsh gaze on Ayaan.

"Stop thinking of Ayaan as the killer, Dad."

"Pack your bags. We're leaving this place."

"I guess you didn't hear me." Livleen moved towards him.

Ayaan tried getting out of the pile of sharp shattered glass. "I really did not..."

"*Suar ki aulaad,* you fucking shut up!" Joban cried out loud at Ayaan. Joban's hands shuddered horrifically in wrath. His gaze fell on the Vodka bottle and he curled his fingers around the neck of the bottle and smashed it on the edge of the bed. Avani felt a pang of horror as Joban pointed the sharp end of the bottle at Ayaan.

"I will kill you!" he said.

Livleen pushed him on the bed and threw away the bottle. "Dad!"

No words were exchanged; only the sound of harsh breathing ran in the room. Every eye was dilated and every mind equally closed.

The next sound that broke the silence was the glass pieces that fell off Ayaan's body when he stood up. He looked at Joban. Avani looked at him. He stared back. With an uneasy conscience, Ayaan left the house in a hurry, leaving behind the clouds of disaster.

The sun had set. A tear dropped into the lake. "Everything will fit right back into their places, Ayaan. Believe in yourself. And if you can't…," said Avani as she came and sat near him, "…believe in me." Ayaan closed his eyes.

"I killed her, Avani," he said, breaking down.

"Are you sure about what you're saying?"

He couldn't answer. He stood up to leave. Avani ran and clutched his hand from behind.

"Let me go."

"Is this what I held you for?" she said. He tried to get rid of her touch, but before that could happen, she jumped on her toes and clenched his lips into hers.

He resisted, trying to punish himself. She didn't lose hold over them. The fight was clear. He tried jerking his lips, but she'd already pressed them in her teeth, giving him a deep cut on his lower lip.

She looked into his eyes and her tongue rolled over the cut, sucking his blood, sucking his pain.

She had made the promise. She wasn't going to leave him.

PART – II

Mysteries are the darkest thing something as bright as love can ever produce.

Eight Months Later

The Present
Green Park Stadium
Venice

You know, life's overly strange when in the end you see your greatest pain becoming your greatest strength. But if things weren't upside down for her, what would she have been called Avani for? And when she finds herself standing numb in between this insane crowd of these loony fans, she feels that in the end, her greatest strength had become her greatest pain.

Folks around her are going crazy to seize a glimpse of the person that has taken the whole of Venice aback with his decision. There is a din all around her and within her as well, but she's stiff. Like an ailing wall which could break anytime from the mighty blows from either sides.

There are thousands of people in the stadium eagerly awaiting the entry of the man who's the reason behind this sudden buzz in Venice, but still she feels like she's standing alone on the edge of a snow-bathed cliff, watching the river of all the beautiful times she had been through flowing briskly deep down, out of her reach. How she wishes she can just dive off the cliff into that water of life again, but she knows that's impossible. After all, how long did those heavenly moments stay in her life, when compared to how far she has walked away from them? Her blood-filled eyes have this itchy irritation that makes her close them for a while.

But the moment they shut, the haunting memories flash against them. The coils of smoky terror cuffs her breath and she thrusts open her eyes, gasping, looking at the huge crowd. And that's when she realizes where she is. Darn! What is she doing there? How can she even stand still? She is supposed to crumble and shatter. She is supposed to think of all the ways possible to end her life that has lost all meaning. She is supposed to blame herself for all the trust she did, till the guilt starts poisoning her from inside. How can she forget her world has broken into pieces? Things start haunting her again and when she knows she can explode anytime, she finds it better to close her eyes and surrender herself to the sore past before the unmerciful present tears her flesh.

2 months before the event at
Green Park Stadium

Half a year had passed since Joban bid adieu to Jagah to settle down somewhere in the backdrop of a southern nook of the country. The past continued to haunt him. Joban would get drunk every day until he would faint. Livleen would, sometimes, drive home early, leaving his work to ensure his dad's well-being and at times he would see his father lying helpless on the floor. He would plead with Joban to stop and Joban would reply by saying he wouldn't do so until his daughter received some justice. And from how the police progressed with the case, his death seemed to be written in the hands of an alcoholic beverage.

Miles from there, in Jagah, Ayaan would still wake up with sly guilt in his eyes every time the sun would hang over his jagged world. He wasn't that strong to flick through the heavy pages of the past. Things around him had changed drastically.

Six months had passed since Avani had asked him if she could stay there with him. Despite his saying no, he had finally agreed. But...

Avani. Just six months and you'll be back. Go and let your parents' dreams be reality. A mere one hundred and eighty days and you'd be back here with the degree.

Avani and Ayaan. Dr Avani and Ayaan. I see no difference. Just go, idiot!

But for Avani, those six months were null without him. They felt as dark as void, like a sleep without dreams, eyes without sight, words without meaning.

She now had her plans set. She would land in Sheher, then the cab would drive her to her hotel, then she would chat with Ayaan lying about her extension in the hostel for six more months, then she'd ask him if like every Sunday he'd be going to Carlton Old age Home, and the next morning she'd stand on the path and ask him for a lift. The surprise she was going to give Ayaan, she could not wait. She had dreamed about how he would peer at her, how she would smile at him, how the brisk wind would begin crawling, how his scent would cajole her into embracing him in her arms. She would think about it with every passing second and each time she would end up creating a new scene. The places would change, the expressions would differ, and everything would feel new every time she'd think about it. The only thing that wouldn't change was the way she would be seduced.

She looked out from the window. Her flight was about to descend.

She entered Jagah. Things hadn't changed much. It all looked familiar. She hadn't been in touch with Ayaan for those six months as he wouldn't allow her to be distracted from her goals. But now, being back to the place she felt she belonged to, she wished he was the same as well.

She'd seen her need in his eyes. He was broken and so was she. She knew how much he loved her and that was the reason she'd planned to live with him for the rest of her life, settling in Jagah.

Though at times she got nervous about this idea, she convinced herself she had no other choices in her bag. She didn't have a family, she didn't have people to share things with, and most importantly, she did not have any reason to not give herself to him.

"Ma'am, here is your hotel," the driver said.

Avani checked into her room and lay on the bed. She had decided to take some rest until the evening took over from daytime. She was about to execute her plan; there was a childish impulse in her to do everything quickly. But she didn't want any glitch to ruin it. After all, she was going to see him after six long months.

So she logged into her social media account and to make things look casual, she waited for Ayaan to come online instead of calling him. And finally, when he did, she waited for him to ping her.

Hi!

He typed.

Hi! How are you?

Umm, Avani, where are you right now?

Her eyes peered at his text unbelievably. For one instant, she thought he knew where she was, but then she knew it was a general question that demanded not to be answered oddly.

Hostel. Why?

You alright?

Ayaan, why are you asking such things?

No, nothing. It's just that I am seeing you online after so long.

Damn, I am so dumb. I should have called him instead. Shit!

Busy with my studies these days, she replied.

I miss you here, he wrote.

You'll have to keep doing that for six more months.

But you said your training would end soon.

It has been extended for our batch for a reason. I will tell you later, Avani made up.

Are you alright for real?

Yes, man! By the way, when you go to Old Age Home tomorrow, give them love from my side as well.

I will. But where's my love, he asked.

You'll have it after six months.

Waits

Okay. Got to go. See you soon. Bye!

She logged out without waiting for his reply. She just hoped she had made no mistakes and as of then, she was assured she had made none.

The plan had been set. It was going to happen the next day. After so long, she would see a colossal curve on his face and that was what kept her lips curved for the rest of the sleepless night.

Avani bolted down the stairs to catch a cab as quick as she could. The morning couldn't have been messier. As soon as her eyes had narrowed down on the clock, she knew she was going to be late. And as she rushed about on the street, her dishevelled hair tossing about in the wind, her eyes with no kohl, she knew she already was. She jumped into a cab. "A mile before Carlton Old Age Home, please," she instructed the driver, trying to adjust in a way so she could see her reflection in the rear view mirror.

"Any specific location?" the driver asked her.

"I'll let you know when to stop." She finally saw herself in the rear view mirror and she couldn't believe how messy she looked. "Just take me in that direction as of now."

"Ma'am, there are two ways for Carlton Old Age Home from here," the driver said.

"Any direction wou…" She looked at her eyes dilating in the mirror. "Wait! What did you say?"

"There are two ways from here. Which way do I take?"

Her head hung low as if in thought. As if getting late was not enough. Now another roadblock had come her way. She did not know anything about Jagah and she hadn't noticed the path he had taken.

For once she thought of going to the old age home itself and surprising him there, but she knew he was shy enough not to react to her surprise in front of a crowd. "Which one of them is the least used?" she asked.

That's how Ayaan was. He would drive on silent roads.

"Oh ho, the least used one, huh?" The driver looked at her mischievously through the mirror and smirked. Fifteen minutes later, the cab halted on a dusty path that ran in between a verdant jungle that stretched for acres on either side.

"The old age home is almost a mile away from here," the driver said.

"Your money." Avani gave him the amount and stepped out of the car.

The next instant she stood amidst the dusty cloud that the drift of the cab had left behind. As she stood alone there, she saw a few cars passing by every few seconds. With every passing minute, she got more nervous than ever to face him. When an engine revved up near her, she would turn and hope it was Ayaan, but every time she leaned forward, her wishes would be dashed. Then she would be disappointed. Another car passed by, and her hope broke down. She was afraid she had been late or he had gone on too early or she was standing on the path he didn't choose to take. Half an hour passed. Her gaze fell down, devoid of hope. The cars still zipped past, but she wasn't looking at them. Her eyes welled up with tears, but before they could come out, she heard a car halting.

Her heart skipped a beat. Oh no! Oh no! She couldn't muster the courage to lift her head up and look at the car.

A voice asked, "May I help you?"

The voice wasn't familiar. She looked up to realize neither was the face. It was just a stranger offering her help, seeing a girl alone in such a place.

"Thank you, but I'm fine." The man nodded and drove off.

Tears jumped out at last. But the very moment the hot flow of her tears drenched her cheeks, her watery eyes saw someone coming towards her. This time it was Ayaan.

Her eyes peered at the car, creating more space for the tears to flow out. She rubbed her hands against her cheeks promptly and that's when she realized that they were trembling badly. She cursed herself for being such a wuss at the wrong time. This wasn't how she had planned it!

His car stopped right in front of her and nothing went as imagined, apart from the pace at which her heart was beating. Her eyes gazed into his and it seemed as if time had ceased to exist, let alone stopping. He had a faint smile on his face, his dimple flashing brightly. His eyes were staring into hers. He stepped out and walked up to her with slow steps. But she could see there was something odd with him. "You! Here? What a surprise, girl!" He reached her and leaned forward to hug her.

He hugged her tight. She went numb, lost in her thoughts.

"I missed you, Ayaan."

Though things didn't turn out as expected, the meeting was still beautiful.

"I didn't know you were here! You should have told me," Ayaan said. And the moment he said he didn't know about it, something in her said he did know, but then she knew that was how Ayaan was.

"I had planned a surprise for you. And I failed miserably at it." She frowned, still looking at him, not able to believe she could finally be with him.

"This surprised me for real, I tell you." He smiled at her.

"So, finally, Ayaan's standing with Dr Avani."

"Oh shit! So finally?" His lips curved high and he hugged her again, tighter this time. She was smiling like an idiot and it was happening after so long.

They walked to his car. He went to the other end to open the door for her. "Have your seat, please."

She laughed at his gesture and said she was impressed. He nodded smilingly and sat on the driver seat.

"I am so happy seeing you back." He winked at her and brought the engine back to life.

"And I am so happy seeing your happiness back."

"So, Dr Avani, what are your plans?" he asked as the car moved.

"Well, my plan goes like this. Old age home right now, after that a meet up with those kids, an—"

"No... no... no!" Ayaan interrupted. "Not these plans. Your plan as in... like, how many days you're gonna stay here in Jagah?"

She looked at him hesitatingly. "What do you mean, Ayaan?" A drop of sweat rolled down her forehead.

"Like which hotel you're going to stay in, for how many days and then when will you be returning? I'll make the plans accordingly."

His eyes were hooked on the road and his tone was disturbing her. She waited for him to look at her, but his gestures were normal. She kept looking at him until her eyes welled up.

"Ayaan, stop the car."

"What?"

"I said stop the fucking car!"

Silence surrounded them. The winds stopped rustling. The birds stopped chirping. She breathed uneasily for a while and then she lost her cool. She whacked him hard right below his ear. The sore sound of the slap echoed. His face lowered and when he finally lifted up his head, she was gone.

Her gaze focused on the rosy sky, feet dangling just above the water.

That was the place she had promised herself she would never go. And while she sat there, yet again, she came to the conclusion that promises were made of a matter that weakened with time. Even though Jheel witnessed a comely evening, she wondered what hurt her the most. Was it how Ayaan had reacted to her presence or was it her uncertainty about what would happen in her life if he'd not be with her?

The sun was about to set; she knew she had to think about what she had to do now. She hardly had any money to extend her stay in the hotel. For one moment there, she felt she had reacted overtly, but if he had really cared, he would have called her. The sun set and night came upon the world. She couldn't decide what she had to do. A sound made her turn to the right.

Her heart skipped a beat!

At first, she thought Ayaan was a hallucination, but then she knew it was not. She kept looking the water until the blood rushing in her body started to hurt. Why is he not saying anything? She looked at him again and he was still looking into her eyes.

"Why are you staring at me like this?" she whispered, seeing his eyes fixated on her. "What do you want now?" She flung her hands in the air.

"I want you!" He inched closer to her.

"You want me? Where? In different rooms of different hotels? Or somewhere away from you?" she spoke everything in one go.

He raised his hand near her eyes, making her close them. "What do you think about the worlds we have?"

"Worlds?" she said, opening her eyes. "We just have one world, Ayaan. And that's the problem, you know? We just have this small world and sometimes, in the flow of these sinful emotions, we end up propping it against the wall of someone's trust. But then all of a sudden, from nowhere, the wall shatters and the world, our world, falls on its back, smashing into millions of sharp pieces. And… and when you think of recollecting them, you remember someone saying – embracing the broken pieces would only hurt!"

Her voice echoed in the air. But the moment her words buzzed past him, she sensed that everything had gone wrong. He has just reacted oddly and maybe I'm overthinking, creating these thoughts and sticking to them.

"No," he whispered and stooped over her, leaning so close his warm titillating breaths tickled her eyes. "There's not just this small world, girl. There's another world, ginormous in size, so big that it overshadows this one. And that is the world that matters!"

She was lost deep in his eyes. Her chest raised and fell for once before she asked, "Then why can we not see it?"

"Because it's always behind our backs. And sometimes we feel we can see it, but it's always behind us. And you know what happens in that world?"

She shook her head.

"All the things that happen behind our backs," he said. "We believe what we can see or what's relevant to our eyes, but no, there are things hidden from us, happening behind our backs, lies behind the truths and truths behind the lies, misunderstandings over things that we most understand and understanding of the things that hold no proof of realism. We just know about a tiny fragment of things that actually matter to us. And in that world resides the immense pile of remaining fragments. And as I said, sometimes we think we've demystified it all, knowing everything about that world, but by doing that we're just shoving ourselves into an endless pit of delusion."

He moved his face back. But her eyes followed the movement of his. She sensed how calm he was, and asked, "And, why are you telling me all this?"

He smiled and said, "Because you thought you're in that world already. I know my gestures were not as they were supposed to be, but then, you misunderstood them and believed something that doesn't even exist to be true, claiming yourself in the world that's still behind your back."

"I am getting none of what you're saying." She shook her head mildly.

"How would I have reacted seeing you out of nowhere, standing somewhere you were not supposed to be, waiting for me to heal your wounds when I, myself, am bruised?"

"What healing and what bruises?"

"I was scared seeing you in that abrupt second, standing on the roadside. When I got out of the car I was nervous facing your eyes that had hope in them. The hope of being accepted into my life." His voice stammered at the end.

She moved her head towards the horizon and asked, "And you are afraid because I want to be accepted?"

"No," he halted for a pause and said, "Afraid because how can a homeless do justice to you?"

His words nipped her nerves. "What!?"

"I've been thrown out of my house." He looked down.

Her cheeks ran damp with the viscous tears that flowed down. With every breath, she blamed herself for being inhumane at the time she should have acted like a mature person. Ayaan had brought her to the place she had come with him when they had met the first time.

"You've been living here?" she asked Ayaan.

Before he could answer, they heard the approach of footsteps. She turned to see an old lady trudging towards them. The lady passed her a smile. She returned it only to realize that she was the same lady who took care of the kids.

"Be quiet!" Mrs Bhaskar suggested. "Make sure none of the kids wake up or else it will be a great mess."

Ayaan nodded and walked towards a room with her hand in his and she followed him like a toddler.

They were in a room that appeared as expected in such a building. Mosquito bites reddened her ankles in just five minutes of her stay. She looked around and saw there were no windows on the yellow walls.

Avani stared at the stinky bed and said, "Have you really been living here?"

Ayaan tilted his head and replied, "Yes."

She stood up, leaving a cranking sound echoing in the whole room. Her heart skipped a beat.

"Easy!" Ayaan whispered and they hoped nobody had broken out of their slumber because of that noise. Thankfully, nobody had.

"And you didn't even care to inform me?" She whispered.

"There was a reason," he said in a dull voice.

"And that was?"

"Because. . . Ah! I know I'd sound like an idiot, but I didn't want to affect your studies. Even if you knew it all, you could have done nothing other than worry about me. Would that have solved my problem? No! And that's why I kept you in the dark."

"But…" she halted midway. She wanted to argue with him, but in his own way, he was right.

Words died. Silence grasped the room.

"What happened?" She broke the silence, allowing him to break his in return.

"You're beautiful," he said with a dead expression and looked away.

She glanced at him with disgust. "Ayaan! Is it the time?"

"You're beautiful," he murmured.

"You're beautiful," I had banged my hand on my father's dinner table, half a month ago.

Because it was the death anniversary of my mother. Everything felt so fresh as if it was just that day when she'd said she would kiss me when she'd return, when she had died right in front of my helpless eyes.

I was sitting in my room, looking at her pictures, feeling her somewhere in me. And out of all those photographs, there was this one photograph in which she was standing at a place that had an under-construction building in the background. Little did

I know that that photograph was going to be a reason for me to talk to my so-called father after thirteen long years.

Wondering how?

This is how!

She'd always melt seeing incapacitated people being helpless in life. She'd tell me I had a lifestyle that is a dream for millions. I could eat whatever I wanted, whenever I wanted, unlike a big heap of the population in this world. She taught me that for some, pain is not having their favourite toy in the closet, and for some, it was not having a mother to take care of you or a father to take your responsibility. And why did she do it? Just to teach me that whenever I felt I lacked something in life, I could remember her words. So that I could never stand low in life. She had taught me the art of appreciating the things we have.

And why am I telling you this? Because this is linked to that building in that photograph. When I was nine, I asked her that if we were so blessed, couldn't we share our blessings with those who were not. And that was when she made me sit beside her, caressed my head, and showed me that photograph, with that under-construction building behind her.

"Ayaan, my son, what would hurt you more? Not having a remote control car or having a remote control car and not being able to play with it?"

I'd said the latter, and asked why she'd asked me that. She'd said that there are people who don't have any amenities, dearth of which proved to be the reason for them to live alone. But there are also some people who got it all, just in a poorer condition, and just because of that, they had to live alone, like having a toy but not being able to play with it. I'd asked what she meant and she'd explained that there are people who lack beauty in their appearances and bad people call them ugly, which they were not. They just had different complexions or a slightly different body structure. They'd remain unmarried because of this.

She'd shared her plan with me that as a child I couldn't understand but now I know what she meant. She had this plan of investing in a website with the name 'yourebeautiful.com' where she'd have made such people meet and stay together with each other. Such people who had been rejected because of their appearances in social life. They would have met and known that they were beautiful. And that was a unique idea at that time.

For that, she had fought her husband and asked him to invest in her plan, but he thought that was a waste of money. So he suggested to her to invest in getting an office made and start this as a physical chain from this state than stepping into the virtual world and investing a hundred times more in something that was not so popular in India in those times. The internet wasn't that reliable during that time. At least that was what he felt. So instead of investing in her plan, he took her savings and said he'd get an office made with that money. And the construction work did start, but then, somewhere in between the dreams and the dreams turning into reality, she was lost forever.

And after her death, the work stopped.

It was only after thirteen years, a fortnight ago, that I saw that building in her photograph. And, Avani, it was screeching, begging to be completed. It was not just about all those helpless people, but also about the selfless dreams of my mother. That boosted me to walk up to him and share a few words with him about it. But he was reacting as if he knew nothing about it.

"You're beautiful." I had banged my hand on his dinner table. "Forgot so early, eh?"

"Wait! Are you talking about her stupid plan?"

"How dare you call it stupid?"

"After thirteen years, it sure does sound stupid."

"Then give me the money. I will work on it."

"As if money is growing on a tree. We're rich, doesn't mean we're going to waste it. Clear?"

"I am not begging in front of you, mister. I am asking for my mother's investment."

"Her investment was my money."

"Then do me a favour. Go to hell with your money."

And then he stood up, kicked my back on the threshold of the house, and told me if I was so interested in fulfilling a dead woman's dream, I should show my intensity out of his house.

And you know what I did?

I never turned back to look at that house.

She was shivering. She couldn't even breathe. She was powerless to think anything apart from how badly things had gone wrong.

"Why does it feel as if all the pain in the world has been made for us and us only?" His voice lurched.

"Maybe because that's what our bond is made of?" she returned a question with no eye contact.

"So, as long as this bond lives, the pain will live?" he asked.

Her liquid eyes glimpsed his agony and she said, "No. As long as the pain would live, our bond would live. Let the pain try breaking us and then we'll show it how tight we can clench one another."

"Avani."

He stood up and embraced her tightly in his arms. "But what are we going to do now?" she asked from within his arms.

"As in?"

"We can't stay here for life," she said, unwrapping herself from his hug.

"What do you think we should do?" he asked. She was left with a clueless expression.

"I guess I could be of some help." Someone said from the door.

Avani followed Ayaan, walking through the fussy streets of Ilaaka, a small Muslim village-like town, somewhere between Jagah and Sheher. He had a paper slip in his hand, on which was jotted an address he was searching for.

The whole locality reeked of flesh. Meat strips dangled in the shops as display. There were machetes in the hands of a few people walking around. All of it made her feel uncomfortable.

"Ayaan, I'm not feeling good here," she said, looking all around.

"They're humans too. Just like you, just like me," he said, busy looking for the address Mrs Bhaskar had told him about.

She had told them that they could live in her house in Ilaaka since she had settled in that asylum, hardly getting any time to visit her abandoned house.

"I wonder if we are at the right place," said Ayaan in frustration.

"I hope we are not."

Ayaan enquired about the address from someone and he said that it probably was a few metres away. Ayaan heaved a sigh of relief, though Avani was sceptical.

"Sometimes I wonder what would have happened, had I not come to Jagah with Luv?" Avani said. "And whenever I give it a thought, it gives me goose bumps."

Ayaan suddenly stopped. She halted as well, behind him. He turned his face back, looked into her deep hazel eyes, gave her a smile that spoke all the words he couldn't have said, and started to walk again. A few metres ended up being a few kilometres and they entered in a completely new locality, that relaxed Avani a bit. It was a tranquil area with small unoccupied houses. A place which looked like an unruffled end of a village.

"Here it is!" Ayaan said excitedly and ran to jump over the tiny staircase of a house, white in colour, and small in size. A perfect place for an old lady with no family.

"Finally!" Avani smiled and walked towards him.

"Give me the key."

"So excited that you forgot the keys are with you?" She grinned.

"Oh, sorry!"

"But..." she said, climbing one of the three stairs leading to the threshold of the house, "the gate isn't locked."

Ayaan looked at the door handle with shock. He re-checked the house number, and confirmed it to be the same.

"Let's knock on the door," Avani suggested.

Ayaan nodded and knocked the door gently. No response. He looked at Avani and she asked him to knock on the door firmly again. Ayaan slapped the door repeatedly.

"Who's there?" They heard a girly voice coming from inside. "Just wait!"

A girl opened the gate. She was tall with a twine-thin sculpted figure. Her waist was tapered and she had a burnished complexion. A pair of arched eyebrows looked down at sweeping eyelashes. Her enticing, constellation-blue eyes gazed at him over her puffy, heart-shaped lips.

Ayaan smiled at her.

"Yes?" she enquired in a honeyed voice, tilting her head.

"Is it Mrs Bhaskar's residence?" Ayaan asked.

"Yes, it is." She raised a brow and smiled. "But she doesn't live here anymore."

"Oh ya, we know that," Avani said, "But may we know who you are?"

"I am Israt Khan, the grand-daughter of her family friend," she answered exquisitely. "And you?"

"Mrs Bhaskar sent us here with the keys. She told that the house would be vacant for us to live in," Avani said.

"Oh, is it?" She grinned. "Actually, she'd given me the duplicate keys because I have my college in Sheher. My home is miles away from here so whenever I have the private examinations, I stay here."

Avani wore a glum expression.

"Okay, that's fine! If we knew about it, we would have come after your exams," Avani said and looked at Ayaan, who looked tired.

"I think we'll have to stay in Jagah for a few more days," Avani whispered. He didn't respond.

"Thank you, Israt." Avani passed a smile and went down the stairs. She looked at Ayaan who still stood on the threshold and signalled to him to move. He nodded vaguely, but as he turned to walk down, Israt asked them to stop.

Ayaan looked at her. She asked, "Are you guys a couple?"

Before Avani could say anything, Ayaan said, "No! She is my sister."

Avani was completely clueless about what Ayaan was thinking.

"Brother and sister looking for a house?" Israt shrugged.

"We just had a dispute with our parents so we thought of staying here until things sort out."

"Oh, I am so sorry."

"It's okay," Ayaan said.

"By the way, the hall's my bedroom and the real bedroom is always vacant, so if you guys really—"

"No, that's fine," Avani said from behind. Ayaan turned and as their eyes met, she gave him a what-the-hell-are-you-trying look and got a just-wait look in return.

"No, wait, I think if you're fine with it, we would manage in here. After all, it's just a matter of a few days, right?" Ayaan flashed his teeth.

"Exactly, Mr...?"

"Ayaan," he said and shook hands with her. "And she's Avani."

Avani gave her an awkward smile.

"Why did you lie to her, huh?" Avani asked, rushing around the bed.

They were in their room that lay coupled to the hall Israt slept in, by a little corridor that opened into the left for a kitchen and into the right for a washroom.

"I wonder if she'd have been comfortable staying with a couple during exams," he justified.

"What was the hurry? Couldn't we have stayed in Jagah until she was gone?"

"May I come in?"Israt was standing in the doorway with two bowls in both her hands.

"Yeah, please." Avani nodded. She moved in with the bowls and sat beside Ayaan on the bed.

"Fruit custard for you both." She handed the bowls to them both.

"Thank you." Avani acknowledged her.

Ayaan beamed, having a spoonfull of it and as soon as the custard touched his taste buds, he looked at Israt and said, "Damn this is, ah, delicious. Wow!"

"Hey wait! Can you... can you smile again?" Israt requested something that felt a little odd to them.

"Why?"

"Just do, please."

"Okay!"

"This dimple of yours is just perfect. Can I touch it?"

All three of them giggled. "Only if you allow me to touch your rare-blue eyes in return."

"Oh, come on!" She frowned and poked his dimple, making it deeper.

"So, Israt, what are you pursuing?" Avani asked.

"I am doing M. Com as a private student from here. Final year."

"So we got two masters in the room. Too much to tackle," Ayaan made a face.

"Somebody looks so jovial today." Avani passed an encrypted glance at him.

"New beginnings, you know." Ayaan winked at her.

"So, friends?" Israt jumped in.

"Any doubts?" Ayaan shrugged.

The three of them celebrated their unexpected friendship with a delicious supper. For the both of them, there was one more reason to celebrate. After all, they could see their problems choke to death.

A piquant smell kissed her olfactory senses when her eyes half-opened from sleep. Avani blinked her eyes slowly, like a lost puppy waking up from a dream. She yawned and moved out of the room following the aroma.

In the kitchen, Ayaan and Israt were making breakfast.

"I never knew you could cook too." Avani made them aware of her presence.

"Good morning," Ayaan looked back at her messed up morning avatar and winked.

"A sister doesn't know that her brother can cook. Wow! Have you guys been living on either side of a house that's like sectioned and…?" She grinned, slicing tomatoes for the sandwich.

"I've never seen him cooking in the house." Avani passed a juicy glance at Ayaan. He blushed like a girl. The way he was cooking or probably trying to cook made him look so adorable that she just wanted to grab him from behind.

"You guys sit on the table, I'll serve you." Israt spoke, tearing the celluloid her daydream was flashing on.

"Why would you serve when we can take it to the table and eat together?" Ayaan asked. There was a smile on his face seeing his omelette not as overcooked as he had expected it to be.

"I can't have breakfast," she said, preparing the plates in haste.

"Why?"

"I am getting late for the exam. The bus takes half an hour to reach Sheher and in an hour, my exam begins." She ran into her room with the plates and put it on the table.

"Listen, sit with us, and eat something before the exam," Ayaan said. "And as far as getting late is concerned, I would drop you."

"You sure?"

"Obviously!" He chuckled.

They sat on the table together. Avani sarcastically teased Ayaan for making the most delicious omelette she'd ever tasted.

"Are you prepared?" Ayaan asked as he drove.

Israt shook her head and smirked. "Who gives a damn about preparation when you can cheat!" She showed him the micro chits she'd made.

Ayaan looked at her in surprise. "Don't tell me you're serious."

"I feel exams are fucking idiotically manipulative assessments. There's no logic in them. Read something and remember it until it's supposed to be scribbled on the blank copies and once that's done, you got the liberty of forgetting everything. They don't test our intelligence, they test our memory." She spoke in one go.

"Woah woah! You seem really mad, eh?"

"I hate anything that makes me feel ignored and insulted."

And before Ayaan could ask how something like exams made her feel insulted or ignored, he saw her taking out a cigarette.

"You smoke?"

"Just because I am a girl, I can't?" she said, puffing her cigarette like its intense lover.

"That isn't my point. What I mean to say is... is, like, you're quite different from what you seem." He looked into her eyes as if trying to seek everything he could.

"Here!" She pointed at a red building overshadowed by the array of pine trees. "That's my college."

"All the best," Ayaan wished her as she got out of the car.

"Thanks," she acknowledged. "And by the way, I am poison bottled up in a beer can."

Ayaan sensed her words to be the reply to his comment. He grinned and kept his gaze affixed at her until she vanished somewhere into the red building.

The moonlight pushed the twilight away and Avani rushed around the room. She swept the drops of sweat off her face for yet another time, but that wasn't going to lessen her worries. Ayaan had promised to be back right after dropping Israt, but the clock said he was at least ten hours late.

A car finally honked outside. She rushed to see Ayaan parking the car at the end of the street. She heaved a sigh of relief.

"Where the hell were you? And why was your number off? Are you an idiot or what, Ayaan? Do you know what I was going through?" She shoved her questions at him like a fierce current of air as he came up to her.

Israt entered into the house and passed a smile at Avani. "We're so sorry we're late. But Ayaan will explain everything to you. I have to rush to the washroom."

Avani gazed at Ayaan, angrily. He asked her to move into the room with him.

"I am so sorry." He kissed her forehead.

"How can you be so careless about me?" she said, ignoring his kiss.

"Last minute plans ruined it all." He made her sit on the bed. "See, after I dropped her to college, I saw an old friend of mine in Sheher and he took me to his house. I thought of dropping you a message about it, but his house was out of coverage area. And until he let me free, Israt's exam was over. So I decided to pick her up on the way back. And then from nowhere, she planned a movie. I'd switched off the cell phone there and then almost forgot to turn it on again. And finally, in the evening when we were returning, the tyre punctured and we had to visit a mechanic."

"At least I should have been informed."

"Should I stand in the corner?" he said making an innocent face.

"Idiot," she smiled and hugged him.

"And by the way, I think we are running out of money. What should we do?"

"I'll have to wait until somebody hires me for their project. But why don't you join a clinic in Jagah as of now until I get my deal."

"Do you think it's that easy?"

"One of my friend's brothers has a clinic there. I will talk to him."

"I hope the wind soon blows our blues away," Avani said and leaned on his shoulder. Ayaan patted her head.

*A*nd you… you are a serpent that would look up to gulp anyone who tries to feed her. You're a bunch of negativity. And even negative attracts positive, but you're one of your uncanny kind, such negativity that only pulls more and more negatives towards it. Oh miss, this world has been made for people who create or who destroys. But you, you are both. The destroyer of creators and the creator of destroyer. Look back and see your worthless life. What all have you done in it? Killed you mother? Killed your father? Proven to be a reason in the ruthless death of your best friend? Sometimes I wonder how shameless you are to even breathe. Why don't you let people live? But enough with your savagery. This man, don't look at him as your prey. I wouldn't let more constructive hearts die in the arms of negativity. Hahaha! I will take him away from you, so far away that you would yearn for him with a hungry stomach, but I wouldn't let you eat yet another gem. Your time is over. Get ready to starve to death, you witch. He will leave you. He will leave you. I will make him leave you. Hahahahaha. Wait, don't run away from truth. There's still too much left to be told. You would suffer, I tell you. He will not just leave you, he would make sure there's no one else than him to catch you and when you'll fall, he too would leave you. But wait, eh, you already have no one other than him to catch you anyway. You've eaten all of them already. I feel bad! Oh, don't run. Just listen, you jinx. Hey! Stop! STOP! HAHAHAHAHA!

Avani woke up with a horrific gasp, her forehead drenched in thick, warm sweat. Fear inhibited her movements, but she still found enough strength to look around, trying to get a sense of where she was. With a sigh, she saw that it was her room. It had been a dream. No, a nightmare. But it had felt real. It began to make her wonder.

It was a moonless night. She turned to her left. Ayaan wasn't there. Something inside her told her it might not have been a nightmare. Where was Ayaan? Her eyes welled up. She got out of bed, still scared.

As she moved closer to the door, she realized it was ajar and opened already. She walked with slow steps and moved blindly in the dark. Suddenly, she bumped into someone. Her body trembled in fear. "Avani? Is it you?" she heard Ayaan whispering. "What are you doing here?"

She tried looking at him, but it was so dark that she couldn't see his face. Should I tell him about the nightmare?

"No, it's just that my eyes opened and you were not around, so I thought I'd check," she stammered.

"I was in the washroom," Ayaan said.

Her brows furrowed. She lifted her arm and touched the wall to her left like a blind girl and realized they were standing a little ahead of where the washroom was.

"But the washroom is here," she pointed with her invisible finger.

"I went to wash my hands in the basin of the hall. The one in the washroom isn't working," he said. "Now let's sleep."

Ayaan went and lay on the bed. Avani just sat, afraid of falling asleep.

"Ayaan..." she said, gazing the windowpane. "Promise me you'll never leave. And, I know I sound weird at this point of time, but I have nobody other than you. Never go away. Please!"

No reply!

She leaned her head towards his face to have a closer look. He was asleep.

She couldn't sleep. She was afraid to throw herself into a world that would no doubt take her captive, taking away all her willingness, and then endure a torture that it subjected her consciousness to. That's what sleep had done to her.

In the morning, Ayaan drove her to his friend's clinic in Jagah. She rarely spoke during the journey, seemed lost, scared of the clanging sounds.

"Are you alright?" Ayaan asked, seeing her eyes scarlet and swollen.

"Huh?" Avani broke out of her thoughts. "Ah, nothing."

"I was wondering if something's bothering you."

"What makes you think so?" she asked nervously.

"Um, nothing. Let it be."

She pulled herself back into her thoughts. Even later in that day, when she met his friend's brother in the clinic, she wasn't responding to everything the way she was supposed to. There was something that troubled her.

"Congratulations on getting your first job," Ayaan said, smilingly on their way back to Ilaaka. "Morning to evening, seven days a week. Wouldn't that be hectic?"

"I'll manage." She wore a fake smile on her face. "Anything for us."

"By the way, uh, I hope you wouldn't mind if I can't drop you to the clinic tomorrow. I know it's your first day, but Israt has an exam tomorrow, and I think she shouldn't be wasting her energy and time in local buses."

She stayed quiet. Even though she wanted to nod and bring a smile on his face, she couldn't. She knew she was being clumsy and unresponsive, but she couldn't help it.

"Avani?"

"Oh, ya! Sure, I'll take a cab."

"There's no cab service in Ilaaka."

"Bus."

'Don't be so adorable.'

"Now, what's so adorable in that?"

"You look cute when you answer while being lost somewhere."

"If that makes you happy, I wouldn't mind being lost forever."

"Everyone's lost forever anyway."

"Now it's you who looks so sexy when you say such things at such times."

"Haha, you're a sweetheart. You'll rule me someday."

You're a witch. You'd kill him someday.

The greatest pain-killer this world has ever seen was sleep, but to her, it had become a pain. The nightmare hadn't visited her again, but she could feel a portion of its presence inside her. She would wake up panic-stricken in the middle of the nights, breathing heavily, and reassuring herself that Ayaan was there with her.

There were times when she felt like a jinx. She would deliberate on whether Ayaan would really leave her just as everyone she had ever loved had.

Twenty days had passed since she had joined the clinic in Jagah. She had a fixed routine – Ayaan would drop her to the clinic in the morning whenever Israt did not have her exams, work the whole day there, and would pick her up and return home in the evening. She had the time to cherish her life then until finally, the night came with its hallowing darkness.

In the depths of her heart, she loved it. She had got all that she had ever desired. A settled life. But like everything, she had her insecurities, the greatest one being the fear of losing what she loved.

Sometimes she would feel scared looking at how close Ayaan was with Israt, but the very moment the thought would enter her mind, she would curse herself for harbouring such low thoughts.

She'd cherish every moment she spent with him. Although, whenever she saw Israt spending more quality time with Ayaan than she could manage because of her tight schedule, she would feel low. All that mattered was Ayaan's happiness, so she would brush her thoughts aside. Israt had her exam the next day. It was the first time Ayaan didn't come to pick her up and before leaving Ilaaka, Israt wanted to go to a party with them. "We're going to a club party tomorrow and we want you to join us," Ayaan had said when they were in bed.

"A club party? Are you guys nuts or what? She has her exam tomorrow, doesn't she?" she replied.

"Yes, she does, but she has already revised her course twice. Also, it's gonna be her last day here. Please?" he requested.

"See, if you guys are sure about it, enjoy your time. I have some important appointments with my patients."

"I so wanted you with us, but that's fine," he said, pulling up the blanket.

"Good night, Ayaan," she'd said after she came out of the cosmos of her thoughts, five hours after Ayaan slept.

The bus screeched to a halt on the end of the main road that led to her house. She got down and walked through the street that had made her feel uncomfortable the first time she was there. The flashing meat strips, machetes in people's hands, the smell of raw blood, nothing occupied her attention. She had changed into something she had never thought she would become.

She opened the door with a hard push. There was a subdued light in the hall that peeked in through the window. She moved into her room and lay on the bed, tired. A while passed, all the time doing nothing. Gazing at the ceiling, she took her cell phone in her hand and unlocked the screen to see a mysterious man smiling back at her. Seeing Ayaan's mystical gleam, she realized something had changed.

The sound was hard and repetitive like someone was knocking on something made of wood. Avani woke up outright. She had slept. For real.

Someone knocked on the main door. She got off the bed and opened it, rubbing her eyes in haste.

Ayaan nodded at her quietly and moved inside the room. She watched him walk away without turning on the lights. Avani waited for Israt, but she didn't come. She leaned on the door frame to see a dark figure walking towards the house from the far end of the street. It was Israt.

"What were you doing there?" Avani asked Israt as she stepped into the gloomy hall.

She said nothing and went to bed. Avani wondered what had gone wrong. She closed the door and turned on the lights of the hall.

"Israt, is everything alright?" She sat beside her bed.

Israt had covered herself with a blanket from head to toe. Avani sat there for a little while, waiting for her to answer, but in vain. She turned off the lights and went to Ayaan.

Ayaan was sitting on the corner of the bed with his head hanging low.

"Are you fine?" she asked him, caressing his head.

He didn't say anything. She rolled her eyes and sniffed before stooping towards his mouth. "Did you drink at the party?"

Ayaan nodded, taking his time.

"I think it's a hangover! Did you guys drink too much?"

He shook his head.

"You need some rest, Ayaan," she said, looking into his pale eyes that were still cemented over the walls.

He shifted his weight back and lay on the bed. She pulled a blanket over him.

She wasn't a dolt to not be able to tell the difference between exhaustion and tension, but as she lay on the bed beside him, she believed she'd convinced herself that it was the prior one.

Shards of glass poked the backs of his eyeballs, desert overtaking his mouth. As he half-opened his eyes in the morning, his limbs felt heavy and unresponsive. Avani came into the room with a plate full of garnished rice in her hand.

"Good morning," she greeted. "Get up, get ready, have your breakfast, and then go to drop Israt."

"Where are you going?" he asked, his voice gravelly.

"Bus stop. I need to reach the clinic early today."

"I'll drop you."

"Don't you remember Israt has an exam today?"

"She can take a bus," he said and went into the washroom.

She wondered if something had gone wrong between them and went to ask Israt. But before she could have asked her anything, she saw her opening the door, all set to leave for her exam.

"Israt!" she called her from behind , but in vain. She'd already gone.

Her doubts died drowning in the brook of assurance. Surely there was something that was pinching both of them, but Avani preferred to wait for the explanation than probing why, what, when, how, on him the moment he came out of the washroom.

She silently noticed his actions and reactions; they were unlike his normal self. There was a blend of choler, frustration, sloppiness, and haste in everything he was doing. Even when they reached the clinic, he drove off even before she had rightly closed the door.

"Hey, wait!"

"Yes?" he asked if there was something very important.

"Ah, no. I want to talk about something, but I think we can do that in the evening." She faked a smile. He drove off. Standing alone on the road, she waited for the car to vanish from her sight before entering the clinic.

But the moment she stepped in, no matter how hard she tried, she couldn't make her mind go the way her work demanded. All her worries, doubts, confusions and fears were walloping her head from within. And that was why she left the clinic an hour before the expected time. She took a bus to Ilaaka. She rushed home and the moment the door opened, her eyes searched for Ayaan. She wanted answers, and she wanted them badly.

"Ayaan?" she called for him but nobody answered. He wasn't in the hall. She went into their room and he wasn't there as well. Badly confused about his whereabouts, she took her cell phone out to call him, while stepping out of the room into the alley.

But before she went on to dialling the number on the screen, she saw something so horrific that it froze her blood and her breathing. Israt was sitting with her body propped against the door of the washroom, with her face dug in her knees that were hugged with both of her hands.

"Israt!" She kneeled down in front of her. "What happened?"

She heard her weeping. Avani was clueless about everything until she saw the marks of wild scratches on her forearms and feet.

"What's all this?" She stared at her scars.

Israt kept on weeping. Painfully bemused by everything she was witnessing, Avani thrust her fingers in the cavity between her knees and her face and pushed her chin up.

And the dead moment she saw her face, Avani shook in terror. Her heart jumped in her throat and choked.

"What's this?" she asked, peering at her scarred face.

Israt closed her eyes tight, tears spilling out of them, falling on the wound, making her squall in pain.

"Why don't you speak?"

She opened them, slowly, to show Avani the pain flowing in them.

"Israt, should I bring you some wa—"

"Your brother raped me!"

Disbelief filled her mind. Her conscience involved itself in a brawl and her mind strived hard to convince her heart of something it wasn't certain of.

Avani's blood stopped rushing for a moment and when it resumed, it ran cold. The colour drained from her face as she stared at Israt's wounds.

She tried to put some effort to say something, but it came out raspy, barely audible. Her eyes welled up as she saw Israt covered in blood. She opened her mouth to speak again, but before she could, she could feel her stomach feeling awry. She sealed her mouth with her hands and pushed herself into the washroom. She puked.

She took her time before settling back and facing Israt again. Her mouth was dry and her body trembled with fear and weakness. Israt was still curled up in the corner, her gaze deadly fixed on the wall behind Avani.

"Is… Israt—" Avani spluttered.

No response. "Look at me please," Avani said and leaned forward to clench her arms tight and draw her attention to her.

Israt moved her head numbly towards her and looked into Avani's eyes. "Tell me it's all a lie. Te… tell me everything wil be normal. It's a lie, no? Isn't it?" Her eyes couldn't hold her tears anymore and she broke into sobs – slow, painful, and drastic. But she couldn't break. She took a deep breath in and wiped her tears off. "I have already had enough of it in my life. I can't bear any more. I know you're lying. I know Ayaan could never—"

"Add one reason to your statement and I would smilingly accept I am lying," Israt finally spoke something precisely in a way Avani was wishing to not hear from her. "And not only me, these scars, these wounds, they all would accept that they're lying."

"And add one reason to your claim and I would fight him for you," Avani said, vaguely sure about the thing she was saying.

"Proof?" Her head fell on her shoulder for a tilt as if she'd lost the vigour of her body. "No. I can't prove it. Not because I don't need to, but because you know it. This all started with last night's party. Going there was my biggest mistake." A dead drop of water rolled down Israt's cheek.

But no matter how hard Avani tried to resist, she ended up pushing herself into thinking about the changes she'd seen in Ayaan after the night's party. She couldn't run away from admitting that he had gotten more aggressive, more arrogant, and more ignorant than she had ever seen him.

"What happened in that party? Huh?" Avani asked. Israt closed her eyes tight.

Things hardly went in her favour. She saw Israt struggling to open her injured mouth to speak and in a light voice, she said, "He mistook me for something else. Something very different from who I am."

"What do you mean?" Avani was rapid but Israt wasn't. She took a lot of time to understand what Avani said.

"I admit I am a far cry from what I look," Israt said in a wrecked tone, barely audible. "I admit I smoke, I drink, and I even behave in a way that stereotypes boycott when it comes from a girl, but that doesn't mean I'm a whore. Does that? And even last night, I drank, certainly half as much as him, but yes, I was drunk. But not as much to be unable to differentiate between his lust and love."

"Lust and love? What are you talking about?"

"He came up to me and went on his knees in the middle of the party. He proposed to me in front of everyone. And you know what I did? I rejected him. As I said, I wasn't drunk enough to not be able to tell the difference between love and lust." Avani felt an excruciating stab in her throat.

"He… he must, he must have been drunk and that's why, I mean…"

"I knew that and that's why I didn't react in the night. I was just taken aback, tired and disappointed. But things went wrong when I returned from college," Israt spoke dully, hardly able to react to her own words. "He came up to me and apologized. But that was an apology just in name. He was rough. I couldn't hold my temper and slapped him for that and that's when he pushed me into a corner. He started saying things that I hardly understood, that… that he would teach me a lesson, and that for him, his every breath was an illusion and he was not afraid to do whatever he could. Because he believed everything would end and he said that before it all ends, he'd make sure my end gets painful. And before I knew it, at this very place, he—" A thick stream of tears rolled down her cheeks and she almost fainted in Avani's arms.

"Get away from me, you bitch!" Avani pushed her away. "Ayaan can never do that, you understand?"

"Your brother is a psychopath,"' Israt struggled, helplessly prone on the floor. "I've seen him change in seconds. I have seen him falsely justifying his presence in the main hall in the nights when he thought I was asleep, but I wasn't. He has destroyed my life, my career, my dreams, and one day when he would destroy your family, you'll know."

❖

This man, don't look at him as your prey. I wouldn't let more constructive hearts die in the arms of negativity. He'll leave you. I'll make him leave you.

When she walked towards the dead end of the road, watching the screen of her cell phone, she could not help but estimate the magnitude of the terror flowing in her. There were fifty-two missed calls from Ayaan and she couldn't attend to even one of them.

Ayaan's name flashed on her cell phone's screen for the fifty-third time in the day. Her fingers shuddered as she swept the screen to pick up his call.

"Hello?" she said with a parched throat.

"Hello? Avani? Where were you? I've been calling you since an hour and you haven't answered! Where the hell are you?" His tense and anxious words thundered Avani.

"What happened, Ayaan?"

"What happened? You're not in your clinic and you're not attending calls and you ask me what happened? Don't tell me you reached home."

"Why?"

"Where are you right now?"

"Ilaaka."

"At home?"

"No, just reached," she lied. She felt like crying her heart out, but something told her that everything was going to be fine.

"Listen to me very carefully. Don't go home. Just come to the Sheher bus stand. I am here."

"Anything wrong?" Avani tried to decipher things.

"Please do as I say for now, please."

"I am coming," Avani said, sensing something fishy. Very fishy.

She told herself that she should go straight up to him and demand her answers. But the very next moment a voice echoed in her head.

I'll take him away from you. He'll leave you. HAHAHAHAHA!

Avani sat in the bus on her way to Sheher. She looked lost and shifted uncomfortably in the little space she had amongst the villagers, their goats, sheep, and luggage. Her bus halted at Sheher. If it wasn't the last stop, she would have forgotten to get down there. It took some time for the bus to unload and after everyone had alighted, she stood up and left. She was in no hurry to meet Ayaan.

He would make sure there's no one else than him to catch you and when you'll fall, he too would leave you.

A crisp streak of light nipped at her eyes as she stepped into the busy station of Sheher. Everything seemed blurred and she had to squint to make sure she wouldn't collide with someone. The loud din around made it even harder for her to understand anything, and all of a sudden, she started to feel weak. The sounds echoed in her head, making her feel sick.

Where's my luggage?

Hey you, walk to the side.

What's the price of the ticket?

My station… Mom, here is… Pocket… Jagah… One ticket for…

Whoomp!

It was dark. Very dark. Her eyes were shut and she lay sprawled at the bus stand like a dead body. And it wasn't like she didn't know. She did. But her limbs felt so weak that she had trouble moving. There were no voices, just the rough sound of her breathing. And slowly the voices started to come back.

Somebody call an ambulance.

What happened to her? Don't walk near her, she's dead.

Hey, side, all of you. Move away. I know her…

I know her... Avani?

A voice broke into her head as the thin stream of cold water splashed against her face. She opened her eyes and after a second of gloom, things appeared clear to her. There were people standing around her, looking at her with disbelief, light passing through them over her face, and someone kneeled right ahead of her, whose hands supported her shoulder.

"You? Here?" Avani asked as she looked at that person with sheer incredulity.

"Yes, me. Stand up, Avani, and walk. You'll have to live. You can't give up like me."

"You never gave up, Luv. You were taken away. Help me please."

"I can't. You'll have to do it on your own. But you will have to do it. Your life's hard, but remember – toughness defines strength."

"Luv. Luv! I need you, please."

"Ma'am? Ma'am? Are you alright?" Avani felt the girl jerk her body and as she shook her head and came to her senses, she realized that it was a mere chimera.

Avani nodded and with the help of the girl, she stood up. "Thank you."

"Where do you want to go?" the girl asked.

"I am looking for someone and he is…" she said and swivelled her neck all over to look for Ayaan. At last, her eyes spotted him. He was standing at the corner of the station with worry all over his face. "There he is."

"That man in the blue shirt?" The girl pointed towards Ayaan.

Avani nodded. "Okay, let me help you get there," the girl said helping her walk.

"Avani? Why did you take so long? Do you have any idea how long I have been waiting for you?"

"Easy, sir." The girl standing beside Avani instructed. "She had fainted."

"Fainted?" Ayaan looked at Avani with questioning eyes, as if choosing to faint was in her hands.

Avani avoided eye contact. She stepped back a little and said, "I've not had anything since morning, so maybe."

"Thank you so much for the help." Ayaan bowed and the girl left. Avani, for the second time, felt left-alone with Ayaan the moment that girl left. First one being when Livleen and Luv had left her alone with him on the first day at the Jagah railway station. That was a very strange feeling for her and after a little effort, she finally managed to brush it off.

"Why did you leave the clinic so early today?" Ayaan asked.

"I was not feeling well."

"And you weren't even picking up my call. I was at your clinic and you were not there."

"So, why did you come to pick me up so early today?" Avani pretended to know nothing.

"Did you go home?"

"I asked you something."

"So did I."

He will leave you. I'll take him away from you, so far that you'd yearn for him with a hungry stomach, but I wouldn't let you eat yet another gem. Your time is over. Get ready to starve to death, you witch. He will leave you. I'll make him leave you. HAHAHAHA!

"No, I didn't. But why?" She lied. Was it a compromise that she had initiated or was it the fear of losing him at such a delicate point of life?

"Great!" Avani saw a sense of relief on his face.

"What's wrong, Ayaan?"

"You haven't had any food since morning. Come, let's have some."

"Why do you look so tensed?"

"Tensed? No! Come, come, let's have something," he said and took her into a restaurant nearby. He ordered a soup for himself and some heavy meal for her.

"I am confused. We can go home."

"No!" Ayaan stammered as he said that. "I mean, we're not going there."

"Why?"

"Because, eh... Avani, we'll not be living there anymore."

Avani tried to look shocked. She didn't want to give a hint to Ayaan that she knew what was up. "But why?"

"See, to be real frank..." With guilt in his voice, he stopped his spoon midway to say something, "I made a huge mistake. A mistake that I promise I will accept with time. I just need some time to forget what happened. And I know how confused you are at this moment, but I request some time from you. Please."

"Okay, I wouldn't ask you anything about anything. But there's something I want to know."

"What?"

"These six months when I was in my hostel, did something happen that I should know of?"

Ayaan comforted himself into his chair and took his time before he said no.

"Okay." She nodded and wondered what she was doing. Pretending to be oblivious to something she already knew? Hiding the truth from herself? Or was she just surrendering herself to the past?

"After this meal, we'll leave for another town."

"Right now?" she asked, though his urgency was pretty much obvious to her.

"Right now!"

"And where?" She studied his face.

"Livleen's place," he answered. Her teeth stopped chewing the rice.

The telephone receiver gyrated in the air as it lay on his side table. He sat half-naked on his reclined chair, snoring horrendously. His thick-haired chest looked damp with sweat, the room so malodorous, one could faint. Shards of glass from broken windowpanes lay on the ground. In another room dwelled Livleen, his son. It had only been three hours since Livleen had slept after hiding all the bottles of alcohol from his father's room.

He opened his eyes and sniffed, almost forgetting that there was no need for it that morning. It had become a habit of late, to take in the foul alcoholic smell every morning. Two nights ago when Joban had fatally collapsed in the middle of the road, the doctor had warned Livleen that Joban was at a critical stage and if he didn't stop, Joban might end up with a lethally deteriorated liver. The warning made him pretty serious about controlling his father.

In Jagah, Livleen was at the zenith of his professional life. But after Luv's death, every gust of a breeze sent a pain through Joban's core. So Livleen left everything for Joban's solace. Now, even so far away from Jagah, Livleen found it a struggle to breathe, he found himself failing as a son. Half a year had passed since they set up house in Kasba, a trivial town on the chest of the southern part of the country. Joban's condition deteriorated every day since. Life had revealed to his father its brutish flank; Joban never saw its beautiful side again. And because Joban couldn't see it, Livleen became blind to it as well. Livleen stood up and went to check if Joban was fine in his room. His father was sleeping in his chair like an exhausted helpless man. He inched closer to Joban and simpered at seeing his plump nose snoring innocently. As he had a closer look at him, he saw a fresh teardrop on his cheek. "Dreaming of your brave daughter, young man?" Livleen whispered, mildly patting Joban's turban. He took out a blanket from the cupboard and tucked it around Joban.

That day was supposed to be a hectic one for him; he knew it as soon as he opened his emails. There were assorted sites he had to work on. A few companies wanted their web portals to be designed by him. A secret governmental organization gravely needed his assistance as an ethical hacker and there were a few freelance coding projects. He sighed and scrolled the screen once again to see if he had missed something. To his surprise, he did miss one email from an ID that appeared familiar. He clicked on it the moment he realized the man behind it.

Hi Livleen,

I am sure, like every morning, you're checking your emails and are taken aback on seeing how I bumped into you after this long. So I'll keep it short and to the point!

Liv, I need you to help me with something. What's coming next might surprise you, but see, if you're reading it in the morning, I would reach your town by the day. I know nothing about this place and I do not even have your new contact number to let you know about my location or ask yours. So please come to pick us up at 2:00 p.m. (if we keep driving with the same pace) at the bus stand.

Though we've not been in touch these months, I know you still have my number, so call me as soon as you read it. And in case you're reading

*it after 2:00 p.m. and my call doesn't connect, you'd find us – me and
Avani – checked in the hotel that would be closest to the bus stop.*

*Much love,
Ayaan*

Livleen scrutinized the email again as sheer disbelief caught
him unawares. He read it once again, and then again, and still,
he couldn't make himself believe it. Why was Ayaan, from out of
nowhere, coming to his town in such urgency?

He felt his life taking a sharp turn back into time. Everything
seemed to be repeating itself. He remembered the circumstances
his father pushed himself and everyone else into the last time he
faced Ayaan. No, no, he couldn't see that again.

But he knew Ayaan wasn't at fault. Ayaan had done nothing.
He couldn't let Ayaan feel guilty of something he hadn't done.

Avani wasn't thinking as she was supposed to. There were huge
changes in Ayaan's behaviour after that gap of six months, but
Avani had intentionally chosen to stay oblivious to them. She
stubbornly stuck to her demand of not losing him, and for that,
she was ready to face any situation.

*He'd have done it in frustration, and most of all, he was aware
of his mistakes. He was willing to move away from them, with me.
I should keep holding his hand. We can forget it like a nightmare.*

"Ayaan."

"Yes?"

"Will things get back to normal?"

He gave her a half-unsure nod. A few minutes later, as the
Google map suggested, they reached the Kasba bus stand. Kasba

was a glimpse of an ideal man's imagination of South India. Majority of the people were dressed in kurtas and lungis. There were temples everywhere. On the corner, they could see an array of coconut kiosks. Ayaan looked for Livleen, vaguely sure of his presence there.

"Are you sure he'll come?" Avani asked.

"I am sure he's read the email."

"I am impressed you know me so well." They heard a voice from behind. It was Livleen.

"Liv!" Ayaan looked at him, realizing he was still the same. Livleen leaned forth to give him a warm hug.

"You guys took me by surprise," he said as he bent to hug Avani.

"I missed you." Ayaan flumped his palm on Livleen's shoulder.

"I miss those times."

"Let's go home and talk," Ayaan suggested.

Livleen hesitated. He gasped, stepped back with a hanging head, and said, "I am afraid, we can't go there. I can't take you home with me.'

"Why?" asked Avani.

"Because…"

"Because of your father," Ayaan helped Livleen answer.

"I apologize."

"We understand."

"By the way, your luggage?"

"We don't have any," Ayaan answered.

"So, you're here just for a day?"

"No. Forever, maybe!"

"What?" Livleen asked with a jolt. Avani was surprised as well.

"I'm planning to live somewhere far from Jagah, and what can be a better place than this?" he said, tilting his head. Avani knew he was doing it to stay safe and far from Ilaaka where he had committed a crime.

"And what made you plan this?"

"The same reason as you. I just need a break from that place," Ayaan shrugged. Avani watched him strive to correct the mistakes he had made. She was still ambiguous about him.

"I suggest you stay in the hotel for a few days until I think of something."

Ayaan nodded.

"You must be tired. Come with me." Livleen made them check into a hotel and said that he would have to leave to check on Joban. "I will meet you in the evening. And please keep it. You'd need it." Livleen put his credit card in Ayaan's front pocket. "3947," he added.

"Thanks," he responded, looking down, letting a sigh of unknown emotions out.

"I know there's something wrong and I won't ask you what. I just believe everything will be fine soon," Livleen said.

"Very wrong, indeed," Avani thought to herself.

Avani leaned against the window and watched a bunch of cats walk on the road in search of food. She called Ayaan who was crossing the road to bring her some dinner.

"Ayaan!"

He turned back.

"Bring some food for these cats as well," she said, pointing towards the clowder. He flashed a thumb up in the air.

She nodded and smiled at a black cat that was the smallest of all. She remembered how she had always loved cats, and how every time she would cry as a toddler, her mother would make her sit near a cat and little Avani would get lost in its mystical eyes. Her love for cats explained a lot about her stupendous admiration for mysterious things. And probably, just probably that stupendous admiration for mysteriousness was what wasn't letting her let go of Ayaan. She'd thought about it for hours, and still, she couldn't tell what was still driving her crazy for him. Was it her helplessness of having nobody other than him in life or were it the mysteries Ayaan carried with him?

She'd felt almost every kind of agony the world had to throw at her, but the one that hurt her the deepest was the agony of her inner crisis. She would question herself the same thing in different ways with every passing moment.

"I am back with the dinner," she heard a voice followed by the sound of the door opening. "And I fed those cats."

What are you doing? This thing is devouring you from the inside. Spit it out, my daughter.

I will lose him if I do so.

You'll lose yourself if you don't.

I've already lost myself.

That's what you assume.

I've gulped mightier venom than this. This is nothing against them.

Drop by drop creates an ocean. You're creating one of venom, I tell you.

Ma, he said he would take him away from me. There would be nobody to catch me when I'll fall.

He is just a nightmare.

And you're just a dream.

At least my existence feels more real than your man in your life.

Why are you going?

To give you the time to compare.

Stop!

The gulp was audible. Her eyelids parted. And there she was, awake, yet again in the middle of the night. This time she didn't shoot herself up on the bed or perspire horrifically or feel breathlessness. She was simply sealed in her position, gazing at the ceiling and feeling an extra weight on her brain by the thoughts that the dream had left.

She checked the time and it was two in the night. She rubbed her eyes, stretched her limbs, and turned to her right.

Ayaan was not on the bed. He was nowhere in the room. She saw a light coming into the room from somewhere. She went straight to the washroom where the light had been switched on, to check if he was there. He wasn't. She ran to turn on the lights but just before she could do that, in the nick of time, she observed a shadow falling on the wall from the small vertical area of the window that was left uncovered by the curtains.

Avani squinted at it and then trudged towards it. She stooped low to let her left eye describe the panorama for her. At first, she could see nothing other than the dark deserted road, but soon, her eye caught a glimpse of Ayaan standing on the far end, on the other side of the road. She noticed him speaking to someone, who was visible to her as a silhouette.

Of all she could understand, Ayaan was probably trying to explain something and from that man's gestures, it seemed as if he was in no mood to listen to Ayaan. She wished that the silhouette moved a bit towards the light so that she could discover who he was.

For a while, there was a discussion and then something happened that squeezed her heart. The man gripped Ayaan's collar and gave him some rough jerks, as if threatening him. She felt like running there and demanding to know what was going on, but prior to her reaching any conclusions of her own, she saw the man pushing Ayaan so hard that he fell on the road.

Avani lifted her face and forced herself against the wall, gasping heavily in fear. She took some deep breaths before she stooped again at the window. She saw Ayaan joining hands as a gesture of request, but the other man seemed unmoved. Meanwhile, just a few moments later, a mild sound of siren struck her ears and she saw the other man run away into the depths of darkness and vanish.

From the other end of the road, a patrolling jeep of cops came. The jeep halted right where Ayaan stood and a police officer stepped out of it. As much as she could theorize, the officer was asking him about what was he doing there at such time and Ayaan was justifying his presence. He was moving his hands weirdly to explain something that Avani didn't understand and then pointed towards the hotel, perhaps to show that he was residing there.

The jeep left in some time and Avani saw Ayaan coming towards the hotel. She covered the gap between the curtains rapidly and jumped on her bed. She knew something was wrong. But what she did not know was why every wrong thing in the world was happening to her, one after another.

The moment she pulled a blanket over her face, the door opened with a creak. Avani heard him entering and moving towards the corner of the room. Ayaan turned the lights on, reducing the opacity for Avani, and now he was a dark shadow from behind her blanket. He wasn't moving, doing something that she could not figure out. She pulled down the blanket.

"What are you doing?" she asked in a gruff voice, pretending to be drowsy. He ignored her question and walked around the room relentlessly.

"What are you up to at this time?"

"Avani," he said and sat beside her.

"What's wrong, Ayaan?"

"We're… see, the thing is we'll have to leave this place."

She felt her head on the verge of exploding. At once, she thought of letting it; she knew whatever she would say, would be harsh. But she hesitated for a moment, deciding to let it resolve itself.

"Are you nuts? A few hours ago you were planning to settle down here, just like you'd planned for Ilaaka, and now you're talking about leaving this place?"

"That happens when you have nobody to guide you."

"Guide you for what?"

"For any fucking thing in this world. Now leave. Leave all this, and listen, we're—"

"We're going somewhere else, again, right?"she asked. He nodded.

"Now where?"

"There's only one place that comes to my mind."

"I hope you have someone to guide you there."

"That's what made me choose that place."

"Congratulations. Happy journey," she said sarcastically.

"I do not understand."

"I am not coming unless you explain to me why."

"I can't think of any reason to fight with one another. That would be so stupid. I mean, what are we fighting for?" Ayaan said, moving his hands all around in sheer alacrity.

"At least it makes more sense than what you're doing since the past two days. Or probably from the moment I returned from the hostel."

"And what will you do here? Huh?"

A pause. She could not reply to that. His words came more as a threat than a remark. "Where are we going?"

Ayaan's last reply proved to her what she had been doubting since long. That she'd lost him the moment she'd returned to the hostel. She didn't know what happened in those six months. She didn't know if he truly had had any dispute with his father. She didn't know what had made him a demon to rape Israt. Didn't she know who that man was she'd seen him with a while ago? *She had to know.*

She had to know why he had made her life colourful only for the colours to fade away later. But she didn't accuse him of making her life hell. His offense was much more colossal. He had made her hell a heaven and when she started to enjoy it, he shoved her back to where she came from.

She had made up her mind that she would go wherever he wanted to take her for now, not to ensure that she doesn't lose him, but a quest for the answers she wanted.

"Venice. We'd go to Venice." His answer jolted her a little, but she resisted reacting to that.

"You're saying as if it's just another town."

"You have the passports in your clutch. Don't you? And we get the visa on arrival. We can leave on the next day's flight."

"Why Venice? This confuses me."

"We have Joe and Kousar there, but here in India, we have no one."

"Where would you get the money from?"

"Livleen's credit card."

"And he would know about us leaving for Venice?"

"I will tell him when the right time comes."

Chinnemma International Airport
South India

After a four hour long journey from Kasba, Ayaan and Avani reached the airport nearly at dusk. They heard the announcement on time; their flight would be leaving an hour later. Avani, however, was not looking forward to anything, only waiting for the right time to get the right answers.

"I've called Joe and he's damn excited to see us."

"That's great," she said.

"He'll come to pick us up. I've given him the flight number."

"Amazing," she said.

Both turned quiet again. It was no surprise for her. It had become the norm. They would talk about something and then that something would be done. Then they would remain quiet until one of them had something new to say. Time passed like a hot knife through butter. Through the glass wall, she saw their plane on the tarmac.

"Livleen calling," Ayaan said and ran his thumb on the screen. He excused himself.

"What was he saying?" she asked when he returned.

"Nothing special. He was a little taken aback, but he was happy I left the car for him," he chuckled. She returned it with a smirk. Yet another conversation died.

Marco Polo Airport
Venice

As the first light of dawn fell on the ground, their flight landed at the airport. It was a fairly new airport, built on the mainland right alongside the waters of the Venetian lagoon. Avani looked at the bench they'd sat on when they had come there for the first time. Emotions had changed, but the place hadn't.

Soon, their eyes met Joe's, who was standing near the arrival terminal. "Ayaan, man-o-man, welcome mate!" he greeted, his voice jovial.

"Pleasure meeting you again." Ayaan nodded and hugged him.

"Oh, look who's adding to the charisma of Venice." He up-stretched his eyelashes with exhilaration. "Ahaan, *benvegnesta* beautiful lady, *benvegnesta!*"

She smiled and gave a warm hug to him.

"Last time I couldn't attend to you, so giving my best to cover that up." He chuckled. "Come, let's go home."

They hired a water boat and everything around was poking an almost-dead part of them into motion. The gurgling of sparkling water, the heights of castle-like buildings, and the smiles of people around.

"See!" Avani told Ayaan excitedly.

Ayaan turned his head at her. "What?"

"Ah, nothing," she said, realizing it wasn't the same. She was not supposed to smile with him and he was not supposed to pay heed to her.

"I know what you meant," he simpered and sniffed. The smell of jasmine that they had felt when they had come there for the first time was rife. "And that's what you were pointing at, right? That very bush of jasmine. It looks bigger this time, no?"

She didn't respond.

"It feels so great to be back," Ayaan said. "This place makes me feel I belong here."

"You do belong here anyway," Joe winked at him.

"Here you go," Joe declared and pulled his hands out in the direction of a house, small yet comely.

"You bought a new house?" Avani asked. It was a single story cream-coloured house, simple in appearance. There were glossy windowpanes on either side of the door that reflected the water of the celestial canal.

"It's our house. And if you guys weren't with us, this could not have come true," he said and pushed open the wooden door.

He asked them to stop at the threshold. "Kousar doesn't know about you guys being here," he whispered.

"You gonna surprise her?" Ayaan replied with a gentle whisper.

"I think I should." He smirked and walked in.

His house was beautiful. The main door opened into a small guest room cum hall. There was a chandelier and below it was a tea table. There were seats arranged around the table in a circular pattern and all of it was out over a thick Venetian carpet. The other portion of the house was partitioned by imperial blue curtains.

"There's a surprise for you." They heard Joe saying from behind the curtains.

"What?" A melodious voice asked.

"Here it is." The curtains slid aside and Kousar could see them standing at the door.

She peered at them for a while before she closed her agape mouth with her hand and sprinted towards them. "What a pleasant surprise! *You*?" Kousar's gladness met no boundaries. She took Avani's hands in hers and caressed them affectionately.

"You've turned more beautiful than ever." Ayaan praised her allure. They sat down.

"Kousar!" Avani peered at her stomach. "You're pregnant?"

She blushed. "Sixth months," Joe said.

"Congratulations!"

"Tea or coffee?" Kousar asked, still blushing.

"One cup kousar would work." Avani laughed, after a long time.

"I am still a little dazed. You both here?" Kousar asked, offering them a bottle of water.

"Well, we're here for a break."

"That's great, isn't it?" Kousar said, looking at Joe.

"But there's a problem."

"Problem? I thought you had solutions to every possible problem," Joe joked.

"Joe, actually, we need your help. You can say we're here because things were not turning out good for us in India, and we've nothing with us right now."

"Nothing as in?"

"Nothing as in nothing what so ever. No money. No home. No plan and no knowledge of what we'll be doing here."

Kousar's facial expressions distorted as he said that. Avani watched her looking at Ayaan with disbelief. Suddenly she stood up and beckoned Joe to follow her.

"They both watched their confused faces before their voices started hitting their ears. Though they couldn't make out the words, but whatever she was saying, she was shoving it at Joe. Her voice was furious, sort of commanding.

A few moments passed by and they both sat there anxious.

"I am sorry to keep you waiting." Joe came, wearing a fake smile.

"It's okay."

"So yeah, you were saying something," Joe said as he sat down.

"No, nothing to worry about. I think Kousar isn't happy about us being here."

"No, Aya... Ayaan there's nothing of..."

"It's really okay, Joe. I can understand," he said and stood up after Avani, who opened the door and left.

"Avani! Stop!" Ayaan screeched, scuttling behind her.

"Hey! Ayaan..." Joe called him from behind. Ayaan turned and shrugged in haste.

"Where would you go?" Joe asked. Ayaan smirked and turned to follow her.

"Hey wait, listen." Ayaan tried to bring her to a halt. She kept on walking in a ghastly rush. She turned left into a street.

The street was deserted, and cool winds were brushing against her rough skin. He ran and stood against her. "I am sorry."

She walked away. "Will you stop?" Ayaan said and clutched her shoulder.

She turned around.

"What could have I done if—"

"What could you I have done? Are you seriously asking me that? You want to know what you really could have done, right? Then listen. *Listen*!" Avani bellowed.

She grabbed his collar and lurched him with all her vigour. "Listen you fool, listen! You shouldn't have changed when I was away from you so that we did not have to run looking for places. You could have agreed with me when I said we could live in Jagah until there was some other girl in that house. You could have resisted your temptation to rape that fucking bitch, you bastard. You could have—"

"You went to the house even after I told you not to?" Ayaan looked at her with eyes that shone with sheer incredulity in them. "Why? Why?"

"Keep your voice at my foot! You haven't achieved something to be proud of. Yes, yes I, I did… I did… I did go thhh…" She struggled to speak. She tried, but failed horrifically. She strove to see the things the way they were, but they appeared to blur, just like her life. She felt a darkness over the light and then… *smack!*

She fell on the floor hard, hitting her head on the ground. The last sound she heard was her nose purring in the pool of thick maroon blood.

Her fingers trembled. She didn't remember since how long, but yes, her eyes had been flickering throughout the moment she'd comprehended she was still an existence. The sharp rays of the sun streamed through the window on her and she could feel the shades of orange on her eyelids. She brought her jaw into a slight motion, and rubbed her tongue all over her dehydrated mouth to feel a taste of caffeine in it. One after another, her senses came back to life.

Her thumbs felt swollen, her thighs strained. Her stomach was normal but a little up, on her chest, she felt heaviness. She moved her hands and they were penetrated with some... some needles? Was she, was she in. .? She put all her efforts, blew some air and it bounced back inside. There was an oxygen mask on her face. For all the good she had done in her life, her brain was something that was in her grip. So, with the count of three, she shot open her eyes.

One. Two. Ouch! Her left eye pulled open with a jerk and it hurt her like peeling a bandage off a lesion. Her right one, well, it refused to even move. It was a swollen sphere, concentrically inside a big blue circular mark, tangential to which a gash passed over her eyelashes. But wait! A pinching brook of light struck her eye. Her reflexes tried shutting it as soon as the light entered it, but it was held up tight. She struggled.

"She's back to her senses." She heard someone say.

"Turn the light off, you idiot." She thought she shouted, but no, the words died in her throat. You need energy to speak. She had none.

The torch got turned off and she felt relaxed. She refrained even trying to move her neck, knowing a slight movement would double the pain. So, without moving her head, she roved her eyes everywhere.

She was in a hospital, draped in a blue worn-out bed sheet. The same colour of the curtains that were stretched right in front of her eyes.

"Can you hear me?" She felt someone patting her cheeks.

Yes, I can, you bitch.

"Can you feel me?" Her pats turned into sharp slaps.

Avani didn't want to move her neck and for all the extreme morons in the globe, that nurse stood as a lone warrior to not understand she had her mouth covered with a fucking oxygen mask. Avani nodded.

"Good," said the nurse and jotted down something on a notebook.

What the fuck am I doing here?

"You need any help?"

Just get lost, you bitch!

"Do you?"

"Mrs Rogan, sir wants to meet you in his chamber." Someone appeared from behind the curtains.

The nurse left. Avani looked at the other one, gazing at her with anticipation.

"You're a foreigner?" The other nurse asked, pulling down her oxygen mask.

"Can you wipe the sweat off my face?" Avani said in parts, struggling to be audible. The caramel-eyed nurse nodded and tugged a handkerchief from her breast pocket. Her slender nose narrowed and relaxed as she breathed.

"A Pakistani?" she asked, wiping Avani's sweat off.

"Indian," Avani said.

"First time in Venice?"

"Can you please call the guy in who brought me here?" she requested, feeling alone and suffocated.

"I have no idea about that," she said. "By the way, I need to go to check on some other patients. I'm turning this radio on, in case you're getting bored," the blonde nurse said, putting her oxygen mask up. Before Avani could react, she turned the radio on and left.

Where the fuck am I?

An hour passed with her waiting for someone to come, but to her disappointment, nobody turned up. For almost fifty minutes, the radio dosed her with more Italian songs than she could bear. It had only been ten minutes since an English show ensnared her attention. The channel declared the name of their first radio storyteller, Andrew Colton. And the very moment she heard that name, it struck her with a sense of déjà vu.

Andrew Colton. I've heard this name somewhere.

And only when he began sharing his life journey from being a small radio jockey at an almost unknown radio station to the triumphant of VTH competition, to be the storyteller of biggest English FM channel of Venice, she remembered where she had heard this name for the first time. It was when she stood behind the doors of Kousar's room, discussing her plan with Kousar's mother. Though she didn't remember precisely, he was defining the term forever when she'd heard him for the first time. And as much reminiscences she could evoke, she could tell – he was dead right!

"How are you feeling now?" The caramel-eyed blonde nurse appeared, parting the curtains that had the same colour as her mood.

"It would really help if you could tell me where Ayaan is," she gasped as she said that.

"I don't know, ma'am."

"Then find out!" she said through gritted teeth.

"Easy ma'am. Anger is only going to worsen things," she said. "I wasn't on duty when you were admitted here, but since two days, I haven't seen anyone come to see you."

"I've been admitted here for two days?"

"No."

"Then?"

"Four days." She smiled. And to Avani, that seemed like a sarcastic one.

Avani couldn't believe it. She'd been in that bed since four days and she didn't even remember a single moment. For once she thought that the nurse was being a smart liar, but when she rethought about it, there was no reason for her to lie. Her eyeballs quivered cynically.

"You please relax, ma'am," the nurse said, sensing her discomfort.

His love had filled the pores of her life and made her world impervious to pain. Little did they know that pain is designed in a way to enter lives. If you block the void, it would shatter the wall. And when the wall would fracture, it would flow much more than what the void would have allowed it. She felt a sudden gush of a volcano on the verge of erupting.

"Hey! Nurse! My head. My head is—" Avani juddered in discomfort.

"Wait! I'll call the doctor. Wait, wait."

She clenched her bed sheet tight, raising her chest, and tried hard to open her eyes. Like last time, her brain was responding pretty well, adequately able to differentiate between what was real and what was not. She could easily tell that the radio on her side table was broadcasting an Andrew Colton story, the ticking of the wall clock, the rustling of the winds, the tapping of the windows, the pain in her neck, and the feeling of blood rushing through veins.

Boom!

Out of nowhere, all of a sudden she felt being struck with something hard. Very hard. Where? She didn't know. But it was somewhere on the face. Her eyes shot open. It was the same boxy hospital room!

The room was bathed in the dusk light. Only sight stimulating rays that she could see were coming from the monitors and the machines in the room. She was yearning for answers to the questions so baffling, they could kill. She desired to cry but even if she tried that, it hurt her head and chest. *Somebody tell me what am I doing here?* She floundered on her bed, struggling to even toss.

"This new storyteller has made many fans in such a short span of time," Avani heard a masculine voice.

Her hands trembled. She flinched in her bed with a jerk, ending up hurting her neck and jammed hands.

"Take it easy." She heard the voice again. She tried moving her neck, but in vain. "I mean see, just two days in storytelling and his show has broken all records."

"Who... Who are you?" she stuttered.

The man walked across the bed and stood right in front of her. All she could see was that he was broad, he was tall, and he smelled of chocolates.

"And why, why did you hit me on my face? What am I doing here?"

"I smacked your face? You serious? I just patted your forehead to help you wake up from your sleep," he said and shrugged. "But I don't blame you for this. That's just a symptom of what you're here for!"

"And what am I here for?"

"To die!" he said, hoarsely. Her heart skipped a beat.

"Haha! That was a joke."

"And mister, that was not funny!" she grumbled, recovering her breath. "Tell me, what am I doing here?"

"For the past nine days, you're doing the same thing. Getting treated," he said and moved a little closer to turn off the radio.

"Nine days? But the nurse said it's been four days?" she asked with a lined forehead.

"Well, the nurse said that to you a few days ago. And since then, you've been unconscious."

"One joke a day is enough, I guess."

"I can joke, but the dates cannot. You can check that anywhere."

As he said that, a cold sensation of numbing fear wrapped her limbs and she found herself more alone than ever.

"Who admitted me here?"

"There was a fellow. I don't remember his name. He waited for two days, but when you showed no signs of consciousness, he left."

How could he do so?

"Was his name Ayaan?"

"I don't remember anything about him. He was not that responsive."

"Who's paying my bill? And what's so wrong with my health, huh? I... I need to talk to the incharge here, please."

"At your service ma'am," the man said and subsequently thumbed a button on the remote in his hands. Sharp rays of white light pelted all across. Her eyelids sealed reflexively because of the sudden brightness.

"I am Marshal O' Brien. The MD of this hospital." He widened his arms, smiling wittily.

He was broader than what she could see of him in the dark. His toned muscular frame was obscured by a black shirt and a white apron over it. His hair was trimmed short. A pair of eyes, the colour of sea glass gleamed behind square framed glasses that kept slipping on his tall nose.

"It's nice meeting you." She watched his small succulent lips parting and meeting to be verbal. Probably in his thirties. Too young to be an MD.

He stretched out his hand at her and when she lifted her hand to shake it, his grip was firm yet affectionate. She smiled seeing him. After how long, she couldn't tell.

"I was told that this was not the first time you fainted," he said and she kept gazing at him.

Avani nodded and only after she was done with it, she realized she almost forgot to feel the pain in the neck. Heck!

"But it was the first time you went into a coma!" he said. "And that too twice."

Another shock. Another lapse of heart beats. But certainly, not another joke!

"I assume over-stress messed up your blood pressure and you slumped. You damaged your head so bad that you went into a coma and when you recovered again, a very rare case, presumably because of over-stress, you drew yourself back there," he said. He adjusted his frames, and continued, "And the time period you took to get out of it both the times tells how lucky a person can get. But your brain is responding to things in quite an odd way. You'd become cantankerous, you'd struggle to bear the pain in your body, at times you might end up fainting, again. Vasovagal syncope, you know. But that's not what this disease is called.'"

"That's just a medical term for fainting due to stress. I know. I am a doctor as well." She pulled up a smile.

"Oh, in that case, you add to my reasons for not telling you the name. It might give you more stress than you can bear right now." He elevated his left brow, tilting his head very slightly.

She noticed the way he talked, bit his lower lip, adjusted his frames with his finger, and did small things that a person does out of habit. He was a geek. No, an ebullient geek. No, an ebulliently adorable geek. No no, an ebulliently adorably sexy geek.

"Sir, there's a problem. I need to talk to the guy who admitted me here. Somehow... anyhow!"

"First thing first," he said. "Call me Marshal. And as far as that guy is concerned, I am afraid that he hasn't left any contact number with us."

"I have it on my cellphone."

"And where's your cell phone?"

"Huh? Well, didn't he give you my cell phone?"

"You've come back to where we started from."

She took her time, relaxed and explained, "Marshal, I am from India. I don't know what you know about me, but all I know is that I have no idea what to do. He is the only guy who's with me and if he is not around, I wonder what I'd do."

"Does he know he is the only guy?"

Sarcasm!

"Listen to me very carefully. Just concentrate on the things that make you feel relaxed. Stop thinking about all those things that burden you. You need more mental stability to recover than any medical treatment we can offer," he said and caressed her hand, mildly.

"Your fees?"

"I have been taught to throw my emotions away as a doctor, but there's this big gap between emotions and humanity. You're new to this country and it's my responsibility to take care of you. And I know, I precisely know I am being a philosopher under the skin of a clumsy dork, but yeah, that's all I got to say." He giggled.

"But what after I get alright? I need to go out and find where that guy is? I feel like I'm stuck here and—"

"Shhh!" He stooped towards her, sending chills down her spine. "I told you to not think about the things that would not even come true if you keep thinking about them. Wondering how? You're in a more serious condition than you know. A little stress can prove to be fatal.

"And as far as your fear is concerned, you can stay back here and be a doctor. I wouldn't mind that." He chuckled.

And after a prodigious measure of time, Avani found herself blushing.

"Rest. I'll be back," he said, turned the lights off and turned the radio on for her.

"She's the synonym of power. She's the mirror image of life. It's she who has created the world and it's only she who can destroy it. She can be gentler than your raggedness can ever feel, but if you mistake it for her weakness, she can show you why smooth floors give the hardest falls. Her eyes speak louder than your strength and her ears can grasp more than you can speak. She's a promise of forever, she's a pain of never. She's the

sunshine in your eyes; she can leave you dazzled or make you rise. You give her the pain and she'll still give you its cure. She can feel more than your senses have heard about and still be unknown. She has infinities of infinity within her and if she doesn't allow you to explore it, just know she doesn't want you to be lost. She'll hold onto you, no matter how far the winds blow you apart but remember if she senses your grip to be loosening, it's she who can create those hurricanes. She needs you for she knows she's the only one you need, and somewhere down the line, your needs are her needs. And when you think she's nothing without you, she'll show you how things can go drastically vice versa."

Avani breathed some fresh air and calmed herself, listening to Andrew Colton. The magic in his voice ruled over her heart and the power of his words made an enormous impact on her mind. After an hour, when the story finished, she realized she came out stronger and a more balanced person.

A little later, Avani realized she was giggling. What was the reason, she ended up questioning herself. Who was the reason, she thought.

Since three days, Avani was putting countless efforts, but she wasn't as concerned about Ayaan's whereabouts as she was supposed to. And she realized it when she found herself shored up against the headboard of her bed, thinking about everything that had happened in the last two days, but about Ayaan. Though it didn't mean she didn't miss him or didn't care at all about where he was, but she had her bars set so high for Ayaan in her life that just merely caring and doing nothing felt like drizzle against the hurricane.

Life in itself is a synonym of chances. And you'd get them every time you'd ask life for them. But, nothing comes for free and so do these chances. So, remember, always take them for someone you know would fit your fingers into his, match his steps with yours and seek all that you need to return to life in place of those chances. Though it felt too early for her to even think about borrowing one from life for him, let alone doing it in real, but somewhere down the line, she knew it was coming. Sooner or later.

Avani heard the story of her life, wrapped in the words of Andrew Colton, who was sitting on her side table, confined in a yellow-coloured pocket-sized metal-plastic hybrid box. She wouldn't get shocked at seeing this storyteller describing just what she wanted to know, in the stories just like hers. She'd become habituated to it now, because she knew that was the magic of that man. His soothing voice and moving words could enchant everyone into believing that his stories were, somewhat, their stories. And he'd done it again that day. After all, that was what she was feeling after spending those two days so lively she could confine her life into them, with Marshal.

She recalled how he came to her room in the evening two days ago and saw her frowning at seeing him so late. He'd asked her to excuse him, but she was in no mood to spare. So, just to freshen her mood, he'd asked her if she wanted to join him for dinner that night and she'd wondered if she was in a condition for that. He'd said she was fine enough to go out and heave some fresh breath into her schedule.

"And where?" Avani had asked him, smiling foolishly.

"Somewhere far from these pungent smells of blood and chemicals. Where you're no more a patient and I am no more a doctor. Somewhere at the edge of moving water where I can see your reflection watching my coffee greedily and you can see a Marshal in water, tearing some bread pieces weirdly," he had said, watching his reflection in her hazel eyes.

"Outdoors? There's no way I am joining you for that. Just look at me." He had smirked, gone out of the room for a few moments and came back with crutches.

"Do I need crutches to walk?" She'd looked at them with disbelief.

"No. But if you refuse to come along, you might!"

She remembered how Marshal had had a firm grip on her smooth hands, helped her to stand on her feet after almost eleven days and clutched her from her waist to help her move. With Marshal by her side, she was feeling warm and secure.

Marshal had walked her into an opulent hotel that had no walls and a roof of stars, moon and the endlessly stretched sky. She had seen people turning their necks to see a girl in a blue worn-out hospital gown, with a head band-aided and eyes swollen enter the hotel, but the way Marshal had been carrying her with him had made her pay the least heed to them. Marshal's strong cologne had been wafting her senses throughout their way and she'd praised him millions of times for it.

"Miss Avani and Mr Marshal?" A busboy had approached them when she was struggling to walk. Avani had nodded.

"This is the table you booked. Please have your seats," he'd said. Avani had a glimpse of Marshal and he was enjoying the way she was enjoying it.

The table, as she remembered, was the best there. It was clothed with red silk, rose petals scattered all over, a candle had been lit in the nub beside which were champagne bottles. "Why all this?" She was still reeking of medicines.

"I told you, you need to be unstressed and happy to get better. I am just doing my job of being a doctor." He'd smiled.

She remembered how she'd been smiling like a dolt on their way back, through the cold water. And only when she was alone in her room after being back she thought about her first dinner in Venice with Ayaan.

Even the next day when she and Marshal weren't exploring Venice together, she had been missing those moments spent with Ayaan there, but not more than she was enjoying them with Marshal. Everywhere she walked, she had a vague hope of seeing Ayaan somewhere, but all in vain.

The way Ayaan had left her alone in a completely alien country did shock Avani more than she reacted about it, but the more she thought about it, the more she pushed herself into stress. And that could go lethally wrong for her.

He will come soon, she'd lie to herself to put a full stop on her thoughts.

"Seems like you're lost in some deep thoughts." She heard Marshal's voice yanking her out of thoughts.

"Good afternoon." She pulled an abrupt smile on her face.

Avani wasn't wearing the same gown that day. She had a beautiful black top on. Her navel was bare under the short top and over the faded blue skin tight denims. Marshal had brought them to her on their second day out.

"You're looking sizzling." He smiled.

"Thanks to you," she said and stood up (yes, she could freely stand and walk. The two-day treatment had worked for her physiological betterment and that was all she needed) and gulped some water from the bottle.

"There's news for you," he said. "For us, in fact."

"Good or bad?" She stared into his mystical blue eyes. She needed to tell him that those red frames were looking better than black ones, but she waited for him to finish. She arched both her brows in anticipation. He stretched out his hand at her with a file.

"Your reports have come and you're fine enough to leave. In fact, this room has even been allotted to a patient," he said and looked down.

His words came as a little surprise to her. She tugged the file from his grip and flicked through the pages, reading her report. Marshal was right.

"Well…" she said in a heavy voice. "So, I am leaving." She nodded with a smile that was always followed by a stream of tears. "So yeah, I am leaving." Marshal clenched his fist tight, nerves popping. Avani ambled towards Marshal to give him a warm hug.

"You're the best doctor I ever saw," she said, snuggling into his chest. Marshal stood straight. No movements. "If we had a doctor like you in India, I would have loved getting sick once a month, at least."

She turned back and looked at the radio, "If you don't mind, I am taking it with me," she said and walked past him, with the radio in her hands.

"Wait," Marshal instructed. She turned to look at him with wet eyes. "Where would you go?"

Avani tucked her hair strands behind her ear and said, "I'd come to Venice for a purpose. I'd come here to get answers to my questions. I need to accomplish what I am here for. I don't know how, but I know I will."

Marshal inched closer to her and stood right in front of her, stiff.

"I don't know what you're talking about but we can do it together. Can't we?"

"Those answers are smart. They would hide in a nutshell seeing someone else with me." She forced a fragile smile.

"Then there's only one way left to do it together," he said and took a leap ahead, his broad chest blocking her vision.

"What?" she asked, looking straight into his chest, avoiding the eye contact.

Marshal grabbed her hair, yanked it down mildly until her eyes met his and said, "By slipping into you." His voice, thick and commanding. His breath brushed against her face and she could smell chocolates. She let herself free. Her eyes closed and mouth, ajar.

Surrender!

Marshal rushed his hands down her back and grabbed her. He jerked Avani up in his arms and as he did that, his muscles stormed into a perfect shape. Avani entrapped his waist with her feet and wrapped her hands around his neck. Marshal pushed her back against the wall. He shoved his right thumb into her mouth and pulled her jaw down, his left hand supporting her in the air.

His tongue explored the cavity of her mouth while his hand rubbed against her silky bare stomach. Their saliva intermingled creating a sensational fluid of love. She clung tighter to him.

Marshal stepped back and jumped on the bed on his back and she, over him. He tossed her back on the bed and clouded over her.

He kissed her face. She tasted of dry sweat, rough and exotic. He cupped her jaw tight and rolled his tongue over the curves of her lips. Faint moans escaped her mouth. She lifted herself, grabbed his shirt, breaking every button that was forming a layer between her tongue and his warm skin.

His body was Herculean. His chest spread wide over his perfectly shaped abs. A holy cross was inked on his chest line. Avani raised her hands, allowing him to pull her top off. Her breasts quivered as they were set free. Her lips formed a crescent. Her breasts were perfectly round, sweaty, exotically whitish and tipped with dark nipples that puckered as his gaze passed over them. His wolf-like teeth sank into her fleshiest parts, giving her the hardest love bites.

She unbuttoned his denims and pulled it down. A gray coloured trunk flashed in front of her, revealing the shades of his shaft. Wasting no time, she hitched his trunk down and it sprung out, erect, facing her.

She rolled her hands all over it, lubricating it before licking its tip. It sent shivers down the big man's spine and he shuddered. Little by little, she pushed it into her, deeper. The sound of her saliva rubbing against it pleased her more to please his soul. She let him out of her mouth and pushed his shoulders down onto the bed. She went on to sit on his stomach and he saw her breasts dangling. He pressed them tightly in his hands, sucking her big dark nipples harder than ever. His teeth clenching them, giving her the most beautiful agony.

The warm passion ran into his body and he pulled out all that covered him to enter into her. Her butt was round, tight and soft skinned. He pushed her down and tasted her. The licking sound felt magic to her ears. His tongue and a finger explored her down and his other hand rubbed her tight nipples. She moaned harder, luring to feel him inside her. He jumped onto her, sensing her wishes. She loved his bulky weight over her as if crushing her to explode into his love.

He rubbed her spot with his wet fingers, giving her the most sensational tingles, and before she could resist, he pushed himself hard into her. Her eyes dilated and mouth opened into hard, ecstatic groans. Both his hands were pressed against her breasts and his weight was onto her.

She sweated all over and he licked every part of her body. Her breasts danced as he pushed himself harder into her. His sweat drops cascaded down his face onto her breasts. His breath went out of his grip and her stomach churned, knowing something was about to flow. And as he pushed all his warmth into her, the two fluids intermixed inside her depths of love.

She had felt his heartbeats on her chest. She'd seen the sea in his eyes tempting her to drown in it. His warmth had made her feel that it could melt her into such shapes that the strokes of hard times couldn't shatter her anymore.

Marshal had shifted Avani into an unoccupied room. It was small and suffocating, but fine enough for her to spend a night in which she wasn't going to slumber anyway. For half of the night, she was thinking about what drove her so crazy towards Marshal and the other half went in her being anxious about the forthcoming day when her quest was all set to begin. Marshal had been refraining her to do any such thing that required more effort than she could bear and the way he was insisting her to not do the things that were more important than anything was confusing her. So they'd come to a conclusion; Marshal was going to join Avani everywhere she needed to go, and she was more than okay with that.

The shafts of infant sunlight were giving her hope that the storm in her life would settle down to be the winds of change. Though she was not very sure if she could find Ayaan, there was something that was pounding her with worries. How was she going to face Ayaan with Marshal alongside her?

This question had been haunting her from the moment she made love to Marshal and she was yet to get an answer. The door on her back opened and she could smell Marshal in the room.

"You're ready to go?" he asked. She turned to him and nodded.

They moved out of the hospital and walked in the streets to get a water taxi.

"Don't you have a car?"

"You are not allowed to drive in Venice," he informed her. "Where are we going though?"

"Let's go to the airport," Avani said and before Marshal could question, she continued, "There's only one person who can help me reach Ayaan and though I don't know the exact location of his house, I know the route to his house from the airport."

"Who's Ayaan?" The same guy who brought you to my hospital?"

"Yes," she nodded. "And more than that, the reason for shoving me into the condition to be hospitalized."

"I can't understand why you are so thrilled to find someone who didn't even care to look after you?" He shrugged.

"Long story!" She gave him a smile that hid millions of anecdotes in it.

Marshal's cell phone vibrated for the fifth time in the last five minutes and Avani asked him about why was he ignoring the call. He stayed quiet.

"I am stuck somewhere. I can't reach now," he said and waited for a response from the other end. After a long wait Marshal said, "Okay, I am coming in sometime. But I want it done, quickly," he said and hung up.

"What's the matter?" Avani asked, tying her hair in a bun.

"I need to finish a very important task. For the airport, we'll have to change a couple of vaporetto (water taxis), but I need to go in the opposite direction for a while," he said and gazed around. "Did you have breakfast?" he said, looking at a restaurant. She shook her head.

"Why don't you have something here? I'll be back in an hour."

"Ah, fine," she said. He smilingly nodded and she went into the restaurant.

She ordered a light meal. The morning people were sitting around her with simpering faces, relaxed gestures, talking, giggling, eating, and most importantly, living; unlike her. She didn't find herself actually living but just spending her life running behind the things that were not going to bring any difference to her past. That's how her life had been. It begins with feeling pain. Then fighting that pain. Getting more hurt during the fight. Finding the cure to the wounds. Getting more pain in the pursuit and it continues endlessly.

She devoured her breakfast that came late to her table. Marshal took twice the time. But at least, someone returned!

"Work done?"

"Yeah."

"What was it about?" she asked as they boarded their first vaporetto.

"Nothing important," he replied with a hint of ignorance in his voice. In half an hour, they reached the point from where they had to take another vaporetto.

They got down to step in the other vaporetto. But just before she could follow Marshal into the vaporetto, she sensed something giving her a familiar feel. She sniffed and a smell struck her olfactory sense.

"Come in Avani," Marshal said, looking at her with questioning eyes. She pulled her hand at him, asking him to wait and moved a few steps away. She looked all around and followed the smell.

"Where are you going?" Marshal asked. She didn't respond to his question and kept following the smell until her pursuit finally halted when her eyes spotted the thing she was looking for.

"Come here Marshal," she said with a triumphant smile.

It was the smell of jasmine and at the far end was the bush. The same on the way when Joe was taking them home. And all the familiarity she was feeling there started to make sense.

'What's wrong?" Marshal asked approaching her.

"If you'd have asked what's right, I'd have said that we need not go to airport. That house is just a few turns away." She gleamed.

"You're content as if you're done with things," he joked, chuckling.

Though, to her, that didn't seem like a joke. She'd not found Ayaan and what if she found him, anyway? Things would get more complex after that! What was she smiling for?

Maybe because she would see Ayaan after so long if it was possible? But why a smile? She should be fuming if it was so. Why do you still love him, stupid girl?

"Let's go," he said and they marched forward.

"Two lefts from here before the second right," she instructed.

"You sure you want to go there?" he asked. "I know I might sound a little weird, but I think you need a break."

"I've been on a break since too long. I don't understand why you are trying to push me away from doing it, but let me tell you, I am not stopping after reaching so close."

Marshal shook his head. He followed her directions and as the paths unfurled, the house flashed right in front of her eyes.

"That one!" She pointed excitingly at Joe's house. Avani pounded on the door with such fervency that she forgot there was a doorbell.

"You!" Joe exclaimed, flabbergasted as the door opened.

"I thought you wouldn't be surprised seeing me here," she said scanning him with an introspecting gaze.

"I am amazed you recovered so quickly the way Ayaan described you were."

Ayaan. That word gave her some relief.

"Ayaan had been living with you?" she asked.

Joe seemed confused at the way she asked him that.

"Didn't he tell you that?" he counter-questioned as Marshal came and stood beside Avani.

"He never visited me in the hospital."

"But he would go there every day with the fees."

"We didn't charge any fees for her treatment." Marshal paced the conversation.

"And where did he get the money from?" Avani asked.

Joe pulled a cunning face the moment she asked him, "I don't know."

"Oh! I don't understand how was he living with you when your wife was the last person to help us?"

"Let's get in and talk," he turned his back on them and moved in with slow steps.

Avani looked at Marshal, confused. He nodded and they walked behind Joe inside the house.

"Kousar was never against helping you guys," Joe said as they all sat in the chairs. "She just got a little furious at seeing the magnitude of help you guys needed when we ourselves are passing through a financial crisis. He's here for a temporary time. He said he'd settle somewhere after your recovery."

"And I am recovered. Where's he now?" she asked, controlling her indignation.

"He'd left in the morning to check on you."

"Why do I feel you're speaking only half the truth?" Avani asked, shadily. Marshal watched Avani as she was steadily losing her temper.

The doorbell rang and their head turned towards the door in unison.

"I think it's Ayaan," Joe said and stood up to open the door.

Avani watched the outdoor light falling on Joe's face as he pulled the main door in. She hooked her eyes at the door to see Ayaan coming in, but nothing happened. Instead, she saw Joe's shocked face.

"Is it Mr Joe Mardio?" She heard a thick voice asking. Joe's forehead gleamed of sweat and his mouth remained wide open.

"Is it the same house this fellow Ayaan Anand lives in?"

"What's his offense? Why is he arrested?" Joe asked. Her heart skipped a beat as she heard that. She tried to move but Marshal clutched her wrist.

"No," he whispered.

"He was pimping. He was caught red handed, being the third party to offer girls for organized sex. Prostitution, in Italy, is legal, but not organized one."

Avani's blood froze. Though she was looking at Joe reacting to things, but her vision was lost.

"I guess you got the wrong guy."

"Leave that for us to decide. And I'm sorry but we aren't here for your opinion. Just give us his passport that he says is in his cupboard."

Avani broke free from Marshal's grasp and scuttled to the door. And as she reached there, her mouth dried. Both his wrists were handcuffed and he stood between two bulky policemen. His beard was wildly grown. He'd turned into something whose sight could inspire only hatred even in his lovers.

"Avani? You?" Ayaan elevated his head as he saw her standing right in front of him. "Avani I was—" Before he could finish his words, he saw Marshal emerging behind her.

"Why's he with you?" he asked Avani from a distance. She stayed quiet. Marshal held Avani's shoulders to support her.

"You fucking bastard!" Ayaan burst his lungs out and centered all his power to run at him. The handcuffs slipped from the policeman's grip and he jumped on Marshal. He clasped his collar and gave him rough jerks. "Stay away from her, you fucking asshole! She is only—"

Thud!

The officer bashed his head with the foot of his revolver. His eyes flickered and his feet lost balance as he stumbled about. He mumbled a few muffled words before slumping unconscious on the ground.

And when his eyes opened again, he was behind bars.

The moon looked smudged in the sky as she saw it from behind the layer of water. Thick tears had been flowing down her cheeks throughout the day and she felt like finally losing the battle from life.

"Give yourself some time. Things will get better," Marshal insisted, sitting beside her.

"That's what I'd thought. Things would get better with time. I took a chance. But what did I get in return? A sex addict partner who turned my life upside down? He beguiled me to fall for him, using my pain as his bait and made out with me. When I went away from him, he felt relief. But when I was back, I saw misery in his eyes. Because, maybe, he was done with me. And that's why he raped his friend. And that's why he met pimps or maybe his customers. And that's why he came here to calm his burning desires. And maybe that's why he carried me everywhere with him, so that if nobody, at least I could serve as his slave. And—"

she stopped, realizing that Marshal was understanding none of it.

"I am with you. And more than that, your Colton's with you. You're never alone." He caressed her back. "But you must be thinking that's what everyone had said before leaving." She affirmed his words within her mind. "And that's why I'll go on to prove my promise so that even till your last breath you'd remember me as a rare word keeper."

She swept her tears away and twirled her neck at him, her eyes asking him, how would you do that?

And he faced her with a smile, replying, just watch me as I do that!

One month later
Paradiso Garden
Venice

The speakers played the music mellifluously. The garden was in the quiet corner of the city, small, yet comely. The land heated up and daisies peeped through the pea-grass. There was a garden pond in the nub and she stood around it, seeing the frog spawn glistening like mini moons. At the end of the garden, there was a small grove of trees of all colours and shapes. There was a farmhouse standing beautifully at the central end, over which she could see a rainbow.

There were about thirty people around her, chattering, gossiping, smiling, dancing and enjoying the party that Marshal had thrown. Though she knew none of them personally, but they all felt familiar. In fact, everything that was bonded to Marshal felt to be linked to her life as well. Her breath had again learned the forgotten lessons of how to over-live the pains of life.

It had been one month since she thought her world had shattered so drastically that there was no binding force that could attach it, but like every time she thought that, she was dead wrong. Poor she, almost forgot the man holding her hands was, after all, a doctor.

She walked around a bunch of vibrantly blooming flowers, losing her breath on their beauty. They stood quiet, smiling together at seeing her brushing her as-soft-as-their-petals hands over them. Even these flowers, she thought, were once painfully closed, showing their boring bud to the world, unable to let everyone know what lay inside. But as the time passed, all could see the beauty of their existence. She could relate to the story of flowers.

Her smile stretched wider as the wind blew rustling against her ears, and again, like every time, out of a very consistent habit, she came out of her dreamland only when the song ended.

A word keeper. Marshal had promised to be and he wasn't so wrong, but a little. A breathtaking word keeper would have suited a little more. After all, he was the one who had given her a life-is-not-about-the-breaths-you-take-but-the-moments-that-take-your-breaths-away moment.

It was one such day when she was helping him with his hospital stuff. Marshal had played a great trick over her psychology, keeping her busy in her interest field and helping her recover. She would look after patients, forgetting she was one as well, and work there with Marshal as a surgeon. Though she lived like a dead body forced into life, at least she lived, and that was what Marshal wanted. To give her some breaths before finally taking them away in the most beautiful way.

She was busy reading the reports when a nurse came rushing to her. "Ma'am, there's a serious emergency case in 202!" she had uttered with a face red with terror. She threw away the file and ran towards the room, seeing a young man struggling to settle down in the bed, his head flooding with blood.

"Oh shit!" She looked for cotton and took a big piece of it from the table. Wasting no time, she cleaned the wound.

"Take it easy. I'll stitch the wound in no time," she said, wiping the blood away. But as the blood cleaned, she found no wound, but a note written over his wide forehead.

This fucking doctor standing behind you wants me to tell you that you give him premature ventricular contraction.

Avani's mouth flew open before she turned. It was Marshal standing behind her. Just when she was to react, she felt something rigid in the damp cotton. She tore it to unveil a beautiful Claddagh ring inside it.

"Will you marry me?" Marshal went down on his knees, his hand pulled out to hold hers. For, maybe, forever.

"What are you smiling at?" She broke out of her thoughts when she heard Marshal asking her that.

"Oh, what? Eh, nothing." She blushed and wondered how stupid she must have looked.

"It's okay, enjoy your time. I am attending to the guests. But be with all of us in fifteen minutes. People are waiting for the ring ceremony," he said and turned back to walk away.

"Hey, listen," she called from behind.

Marshal looked at her. His golden badge over the black coat gleamed more than the white silky shirt did. He'd had two of his shirt buttons open, allowing his chest line to seduce her heart.

"You're looking so good today that," she snickered, "you give me premature ventricular contraction." They giggled.

Avani roamed around that heavenly place. Carrying an everlasting simper on her face, she moved towards the exit, lost in herself, unknown of where she was walking.

Life had taken her on such a path where the pain was just a myth and Ayaan was just a thing of the past. She was not concerned about paying heed to the path for she knew the roads were straight now, and whenever she would raise up her head, she would just see bliss right ahead of her.

She beamed realizing she was so lost in her thoughts that she was walking anywhere. She raised her head up to have a sight of what lay ahead of her and as her eyes looked straight, she saw someone coming towards her. And it was not the bliss! It was…

"You?" She peered at Ayaan who was standing right in front of her.

His face was dry and dark with the signs of dried sweat. His beard was shabbier than it was the last time.

"Hey, you? What the fuck are you doing here?" Marshal shouted as he came running from the far end.

"I just need to talk to you." He flinched seeing Marshal rushing towards him with a red face.

"What the hell do you want to say now?" Avani shouted, caring the least about the guests, who'd already gathered behind them. "You should be rotting behind bars."

The air got tensed and all of the sudden, the eyes that were witnessing heaven a few seconds ago, squinted, resisting the flames of hell itching them.

"Give me just five minutes." He looked into Marshal's eyes, ignoring Avani.

"Answer me first," Avani said through gritted teeth.

"No, wait. Let's give him one chance," Marshal set his hand on her shoulder.

"Come with me in the room upstairs," Marshal said, pointing towards the two-storey farmhouse on the end of the garden.

"Why there?" Avani whispered, poking Marshal's arms. He pointed towards the guests with the corner of his eyes to make her understand. She nodded at Marshal and said, "Even I'll come along."

"But I said just him. Just. Him," Ayaan growled. Marshal gave her a look of assurance and left.

Avani saw the guests looking at her with confused eyes and all she could do was walk away from them, her eyes teary. Why did he have to enter her life when she had found one good reason to keep breathing keeping her sores at bay?

Every minute felt like a lifetime full of vexation. She looked at her wristwatch, and it was already ten minutes since they were in.

Just five minutes, Ayaan had said.

She waited, standing at her place, weeping ceaselessly. Her eyes felt as if they'd swell if she didn't see Marshal by her side in some moments. She couldn't take it anymore. She dashed towards the farmhouse.

There were only three rooms in the left wing and the last one had its door open. She walked towards it and stepped in, only for her heart to freeze. Her jaw fell as her eyes saw the sight waiting for her in the room. A glimpse more painful than death.

She saw a gun on the floor beside which was Marshal, lying in a pool of blood, lifeless.

Dead!

The windows were open, screeching the story that they witnessed before someone jumped out of them and ran away.

She lost her vision and before the floor could accept her unconscious, life stood to laugh at her, as if saying,

I told you I am all about the moments that take your breath away. HAHAHAHA!

Five Days Later

The wall clock ticked in the dark, suffocating, deadly room. The windows were shut and the door was locked so tight it did not let any air pass through. The room reeked of fresh and dried blood.

Sealed between the V-shaped linkage of two walls, Avani sat with her face snuggled in her chest, covered by her bent feet. She didn't remember where she was. She couldn't recall how many days she had been living that way. How big was the room, if it was even a room? Did she even have a bed around her or had she been sleeping in the same position for a reason? And to make things worse, she couldn't even decipher what she actually was doing to herself.

The closest she was to remembering anything was when she could recall her image, failing thrice to kill herself. Three suicide attempts and all of them a big failure. For an instance she felt pity for the old Avani, who was shedding tears on the coffin of Marshal, seeing her big man helplessly packed. She felt pity for that Avani who missed a big chance of getting buried under the same layer Marshal disintegrated into. She didn't want to live and that was true. But if by any chance she lived, she wouldn't let him live and that was truer.

Who the fuck was he to give her false hopes, to enter her life, use her the way he wanted, toss her away when he was done, carry her along as a backup, destroying more bricks from the wall of her life than he'd added, leave her in a way that nobody could hold her, and then snatch that nobody from her life? For her, things still hadn't gone wrong, but now she was going to make sure they did. She was going to make Mr Anand piss breath and poop flesh.

She coughed hard and then puked some more blood. Her body felt weaker and her muscles ached as if they were soon going to give up. The iron door opened with an itchy sound and after what seemed to be a lifetime, she saw light. It, in actual, had only been seventy-two hours since the police had jailed her in the dark cell, finding her suspiciously on the spot where the dead body was found. Even though every eyewitness suggested the police was wrong in its proceedings, they didn't want to take any chances.

"You alright?" A policeman rushed in the cell. He sniffed and a pungent smell of blood entered his nostrils. He turned his torch on and he saw blood all over the floor.

"Stand up and move out with me." The policeman grabbed her arms to help.

She moved her leg forth, one after another, leaning onto the policeman completely.

"Sir, she needs a doctor," the policemen said, entering the inspector's office.

The police inspector watched the half-dead girl as she entered his cabin.

"What's wrong with her?" He sprung out of his chair. She shot up her eyelids and moved her eyes all around, totally unaware of where she was. Again!

"She's critically morbid," the constable said.

A sudden pain throbbed and pulsed in her skull. Not a sharp pain like a knife-inflicted, but more of a dull pounding with a hammer over and over again. She closed her eyes tight for some time and that seemed to help.

"Should I call a doctor?"

"No," he said, seeing Avani open her eyes again. "Set her free."

Her eyes fell on the front page of an English newspaper and she would have ignored it completely if the first glimpse of it didn't read Colton.

"But sir?"

"Do as I say," the inspector said. "We have no evidence against her. The gun that we found beside the body had finger prints of the dead man himself, and more than that, postmortem says he was never shot in the first place. The gun hadn't even been fired! He died because something hit his head hard. What if she dies here? We'll lose our jobs. All the evidence is in her favour."

"*What!*" Avani exclaimed loud, shocking the two.

For a moment the inspector took it as her gusto of imagining herself free, but soon he discovered he was wrong. He saw her eyes glued to the front page heading of the newspaper that read, *Colton bids adieu to storytelling, leaving his fans dazed worldwide.*

"We're setting you free and you're concerned about this over-hyped storyteller."

"Dare you call him that!" she said, gnashing her teeth in fury.

"Was she acting morbid till now?" The policeman commented, seeing a completely new flow of energy in her.

"Collect your passport from the counter. I am setting you free from my side. I shall not be responsible for anything, now," the inspector said and moved out of his cabin.

Her hands quaked the moment she was done with reading the news. The next day, in the evening, Andrew Colton was going to tell a story live in front of thousands of people for the last time.

He was her last hope. He couldn't do that. She had to live, and if there was one man who could blow life into her, it was Andrew Colton. She had to be there. She knew she couldn't stop him, but she had to be there to know what made him quit giving her hopeless lives hopes. She had to be there, for it was the last loot in the mine full of reasons to live. And she was feeling an intense dearth of that. Intense dearth!

Back to the present

Like she was wondering before flying into a flashback, she still is confused about what gives her so much courage to stand in this crowd of thousands when she is the most shattered among everyone? Is it her admiration and respect for Andrew Colton that she has come to show at the time she should have already been a thing of the past, or is it the courage she wants to seek in an all-at-once fashion, to prevent herself from being a thing of the past?

Whatever the reason is, she's there, looking forward to seeing the creator of her hopes and destroyer of her torments. Between the mass of folks, like a crumpled paper in a notebook, she thinks about how she'd react to his first glimpse, how would things turn out when he'd justify the cause of his step, how she would feel stronger on listening to him speak and how she'd decide how to live her remaining life, based on the way this session was going to turn out.

Her never-ending chain of thoughts finds no halt until she hears the mob go crazy at something. She swivels her gaze all over and on the big screen that's displaying the internal structure of the stage, she sees Andrew Colton moving towards the stage. Her heart begins to pound her ribs harder than it ever did under any emotion, and the screen displays the countdown.

Ten, Nine, Eight, Seven, Six, Make, some, noise, for, Andrew, COLTON!

The crowd of over sixty thousand people, snugly fitted in the stadium that has the capacity to bear only half the number of people there, takes the surrounding head on. Hisses and hustles shoot on and if the police weren't giving their best, there would have been total chaos.

But she, she stands like a silent tree standing against the hard hitting hurricane. The moment she catches the first glimpse of Andrew Colton climbing up the stage, escorted by a chain of bouncers, dressed in a black shirt and blue denims over neatly polished shoes, as she could see on the big screen, she forgets she is designed in a way to breathe.

There are thousands of people cheering his name, but he, he is lost somewhere. There isn't that luster on his face, as if he is broke from within. But only and only she can notice it in the place thronged with people full of curiosity.

Andrew Colton looks at the crowd and waves his hand with a smile that she doesn't know why feels fake. The anchors plead everyone to cut the din off so that it can be easier for all to listen to him.

He brings the mic closer to his lips, and even before he can say anything, the crowd goes nuts. He smiles and tries again, but fails again. As it happens every time he tries to speak something, the lure to listen to him speaking jumps higher in her. She is waiting for it to begin, but more than that, she is afraid of what would happen when it would all end? What lay ahead? A colossal void? "Hello, Venice!" His voice breaks the din apart and as he says that, something very unusual happens.

His command so yielding over the magic in his voice that it feels like he mouthed a spell and all of them got spellbound to silence.

"Thank you so much for turning out in such a big number," he says and adjusts himself into his king size seat. "I won't say I wasn't expecting such a huge attendance, but for sure I'd say I don't deserve it."

His statement creates a buzz in the people and someone from the front row shouts. "You deserve the best, champion!"

Avani watches his high cheekbones getting fleshier as his lips curve into a smile. His big eyes resisted a little when his long hair fell on his face as he bowed to them, while seated. Not more than twenty-five, she thinks.

"I can feel your emotions. They're so pure and honest." He licks his lips and says, "But there's a big reason behind me saying that. And so as to let your imagination measure its magnitude, so big that that's the reason I am here, announcing my retirement from a career that had not even started properly. And you know what that reason is?" he asks, elevating his head and his brows in a union. There is a profound silence all around. He takes a deep breath, lets it out and says, "That I, unlike your emotions, wasn't true and honest in serving you!"

Everyone watches him shocked. And for the first time, Avani reacts the same way the crowd did.

"How would you stand when you've got your spine fractured? And could you even stand if you got your spine intact but no flesh covering it?" He shrugs, confusing one and all in the mob. "And that was what my stories were. My flesh and someone's spine."

Buzz takes over again, but before it takes the shape of din, he continues. "Yes, and sitting here in front of thousands of people and millions of them watching me on assorted sources of media, I confess that all the stories that won millions of hearts in shortest period of time were someone's words wrapped in my voice. They all were written by a ghost writer. A person of his word. A man

I would admire till my last breath. My friend for this and other lives."

He pauses for a break to let people recover from what they have heard. "I know you all are feeling cheated right now, but subsequently, all of you are wondering what makes me confess it suddenly, or that even if it were ghost written, why am I quitting my job? And I've already told you the reason. If a spine is nothing without the flesh then flesh, too is nothing but a useless chunk without the spine. And I quit because I can no more stand on the stage to win your hearts. My spine, after all, has fractured. And for all of you who're wondering what in this world am I up to, this story, my last story will explain a lot better."

Dead silence!

"It's the story of my friend, my ghost writer and closest to your convenience, my spine. It's a story that tells many stories in one. It's the true account of his life that unfurls the many hidden truths of my own life and yes… Yes, you must be wondering even if I don't have the same ghost writer for whatever reasons, why can't I have another. After all, at the stage I am on, even nursery rhymes from me might get more listeners than ever, but I say wait. Wait and let this tale unroll the things for you."

His eyes get a little welled up as he thinks about the thing he is going to speak about, but he resists the flow of the water that deceives you into a person you're not. He closes his eye, fills his chest with air around the tensed faces, picks up a bunch of papers from behind his seat, unfolds them to make the words in them clear for him and says, "This is the letter he wrote to me five days ago. Hidden in the spaces between these words, here comes the last story of my life."

❖

Hello Mr Colton,

A champion is not made from the right decisions he takes. The experiences he's gained from taking the wrong decisions make him a champion. I've already had my share in taking plenty of wrong decisions. I hope you're the right one.

Remember these were the first words you told me? I must say that I never thought we would grow so close so fast, but since we did, I must not forget to thank you for being an integral part of my life. I must, uh, wait. Did I just call the thing I am doing these days a life? Stupid me, I apologize. Let me correct. So, I must not forget to thank you for being an integral part of my compromise-with-all-the-wrong-decisions-I-took! This doesn't sound better, but is original. That's how things had been and that's what I was making the life of people around me.

I, Mr Colton, have written tons of stories for you, but today I quit. And as I do it, I give you a reason to quit as well. Don't be confused, but patient. Doesn't the biggest storyteller of the world in recent times know that in good stories things unfurl with time? But how can I break the bond so quick? There has to be a farewell, Ummm, farewell what? Yeah! A farewell story. And this, my friend, is the last story that I am writing for you. You ask me why? You'd know it soon. It's a story of many lives combined in one. It's your story, it's my story, it's the story of our fractured lives.

Mr Colton, I seek your apology even before I proceed, because I feel there are some heavy chances of me messing up this one, unlike the other stories I've written for you. But, hey, Mr Colton, remember – life's stranger than fiction, because fiction has to make sense. And this story is my life, not your pitch perfect fiction!

Let me take you back to the brook of my childhood. I was the only son of a strict police officer and a very sweet, beautiful, charming, sensible, intellectual, deep, warm, and… oh I can go on bragging about my mother. It was a life I would choose to live a million times over and still wouldn't get tired of. After all, I believe, childhood is the only phase of life when fantasy meets reality. Isn't it? But, not always. At least, this thing applied partially in my case. For ten years, it was more than a fantasy, but when I turned ten, after a few months, I lost my mother. How? Well, that's a long story, so I leave it there.

I was shattered, and more than that, haunted at seeing her take such a ghastly escape from my life. Ever since she left me alone in this cruel world, I started digging all the beautiful things out of it. That was the only option I was left with. Finding beauty in the life full of malice. That wasn't an easy thing to do, but wasn't as difficult as it was to live without a mother. The greatest pain you get to feel becomes a benchmark of agony in your life. And only the pain greater than that can hurt you. That's what we call coming out as a stronger person.

My father and I shared no words since the death of my mother because of a reason that's a story left unsaid, but still, I never felt his death affecting my life. Because, I believe, if you can learn to live without them even after being together, there's no separation that can be bigger than that. So, somewhere between feeling the strikes of pain and filling the wounds of pain, I grew up.

But that's what I thought until I met her and every story is incomplete without her. But her in my story is the reason for it being left incomplete. Somewhere between the roads of coincidence and it-was-meant-to-be diaries, my eyes met hers and, Mr Colton, you ask me to swear by any fucking thing in this world and I would do that grinning, and promise she was more gorgeous than the dream girls in cartoons. In the first glimpse of her, my friend, I could see my mother, and I don't know if she actually resembled her or because I made myself look at her that way. I am confused about that, but one thing I wasn't confused about was that her eyes were comely. Those bluish-brownish green eyes like my mother's and what do we call that word, eh, I forgot but that colour, I swear seemed to have derived from her eyes. So vibrant and sparkling.

I don't know why but with every second I spent with her, I wondered what makes some moments more special than the others. She was a life deeply fractured and I was a story widely broken, and we knew every story needs a life just like every life needs a story. We knew we were meant to be the ones for each other. But the only thing that proved to be a barrier was that she was a little more shattered than me and we could not fit in the voids of one another. And then I had two choices from there. Either to fill her fractures with my love or to break myself a little more to fit perfectly for her, and Mr Colton, I tried both.

I tried healing her with all the magic I had and her gaps started to fill day by day, little by little. But if everything opens up to be smooth, why would life be called life? And I was so in haste to complete us that when I couldn't wait for her fractures to fill, I broke myself a little. After all, Mr Colton, if it is true love, it has to have twists and turns for sure. Though exceptions are everywhere, exceptions too are exceptional cases when it comes to love. That's how I would integrate the whole being of our united life. But isn't mystical disintegration the trademark of every Andrew Colton story? So, just to let my last story for you have that trademark, here I disintegrate my life events that I thought would bury in the soil with me. But now as I sit and write it for you, I don't see it happening.

Unspoken words often add up to create the darkest stories. These words down there, belong to this category. And as things would unfurl, you'd know how!

So, Mr Colton, we met in this Indian town, Jagah. She'd come on a vacation with her friend who happened to be the sister of my friend. We happened to meet and like everyone from your stories, we fell in love the way we were with each other. I wouldn't say there was some magic for her or for me, but for sure there was some magic in our togetherness that every time it came, life, no matter how cruel it was, seemed beautiful.

We were together through thick and thin. We'd seen death so close, we could smell it, and life so real we could talk to it. I'd even brought her to this heaven called Venice once and we'd even made friends here. You know whom I am talking about, right?

But Mr Colton, we fall in love just to know what broken feels like. That's harsh, but that's true. As true as it's incomplete. We do fall in love to know what broken feels like, but if we conquer the hard times with a brave smile on our face, and yielding grip to each others' hand, love falls in us just to let us know what being healed means. And that gap between you falling in love and love falling in you isn't that easy to leap ahead. If I would sum up my life in a few words, I'd say that was the gap where the grip of our hands broke apart. Wondering how? Here's how!

After tasting the rawness of life at fullest in Venice, when we returned, things started to fall apart. As if life saying, 'Done with your deeds? Now let's have some serious business.' Her friend, Preet (and that wasn't her real name but every person except one who would come in the end would have a pseudonym), the reason behind me meeting her, became the first crack in the wall of our love, our lives, our dreams. No, Preet hadn't made some big mistake, but just a small one. Wondering what?

She just got a little brutally murdered! That's it, Mr Colton. That's it!

This happened as suddenly as it appeared in this story. It all happened in a celestial evening that I, Rhea (that's the pseudonym for that beauty), Preet and her brother Maan, were enjoying together. Life was moving like a hot knife through butter until it struck against the pebble in the butter cake, and from nowhere in that heavenly day, someone attacked Preet to death.

We were dead unknown about why and who did that, but her demise walloped us so firm that we were stranded to think that it was the end of our life that had begun to reconstruct. But it wasn't! We were wrong. It wasn't even the start.

Within some hours of her stay, the investigation team researched the case and they concluded that the reason behind her murder was… *me. No!* Do not be so shocked. I would suggest you save it for later. And anyway, the reason as in not being the one who got her murdered, but the one who was attempted to be murdered by his foes but their target missed and she got killed instead. Why did my foes want to kill me, you ask? Again a long story, so I'll leave that untouched if you allow me to. You say yes? Oh, thanks. But I say no. No, not to your affirmation, but to the theory that the investigation committee had come out with, considering me to be a lucky bastard that poor girl had to die for. That was not the case. Things were too different than they appeared. They were more complex than the theory all those investigation teams had come up with to sweep off the burden of yet another case. And even I wasn't aware of it until I discovered it later. When? You'd know.

So, as I said, things fell apart and Preet's father, who was once damn chummy with me started considering me as his daughter's murderer. I don't blame him for his reactions. A father whose wife was abducted when his kids were too small to even understand what abduction actually meant, when reacted to the death of her daughter in quite a wrathful fashion, I really was not surprised.

Things got worse when they left the state and settled far away, thinking that it would help them running away from their past and I don't know if it did, but they left me all alone, once again. Even Rhea went back to her college to complete her MBBS, that was just six months away. Those months passed like years, every second crawling at its slowest. After keeping your hand dipped in warm fluid for too long, even the touch of normal one feels cold. That's what my life felt without her. Without Ma. I was habituated of their warmth and I missed it with every passing second, until I realized she was back in my life after six months. And that was from where things began to change.

You know, Mr Colton, in your life only once you have an actual chance to choose. Then, for the rest of your life, you would just be padding the choice that you made. And that's what had happened with me and probably that's where I went wrong.

She'd come to Jagah without informing me about her arrival, planning a surprise for me and she thought she succeeded, but she didn't. A little mistake from her side and I had to turn my world upside down. She'd come to Jagah a day prior to when she'd planned to surprise me and she thought I had no idea about her arrival; she was wrong. There was someone who'd already informed me on the very day she landed in Jagah. That person was none other than she herself.

When she was back in town, just to know about the path she could stand on to surprise me, she sent me a text on social media, lying about how she was stuck in her training for six more months and all those lies didn't work because of her silly mistake of forgetting to turn her GPS off. So, as her text came to me, I could read 'sent from Jajah' underneath it. And as that happened, my heart skipped a beat!

You mustn't be aware Mr Colton, so let me tell you that Rhea was, what the world calls the people of her kind, an orphan. She had no one in this world, but me. I was neatly cognizant of her intentions to be back in Jagah and that was to start a new life with me. Not because she had no other choice, but because I was not a choice to her. I was a reason. A reason for her to breathe on and on.

But Mr Colton, I knew though my father had no interest, what so ever, in my life, he was still not going allow me to marry a girl of my choice. He could kill people to satisfy his ego, let alone rejecting the girl I loved. I knew her instant arrival could prove to be a hindrance in our relationship and so I was left with two options to chose from. Either I could run away from my house or ask my father's approval. And I chose the prior one.

And that's the decision I was padding up until now. Oh, I was such a failure at choosing that and I still regret. But I couldn't see her feeling guilty about her presence in my town, so I lied making up a story about how my father had thrown me out of my house.

Like it should have happened, she believed it and I thought the hard times would face cessation. I was wrong, yet again. Do you know, Mr Colton, why every time when you think things are getting back to their place, life disarranges every space of it? Do you? If you do, I wish I would have met you earlier to know. I think many misunderstandings could have been evaded. Just like the one that happened between us, after we left Jagah to start a new life!

So, forgetting all that, I swallowed to reach that point in life. I began the new chapter of my book with her, in a small town somewhere near Jagah. We chose that place for we needed a house to live in and my dearest aunt had one in that town, unoccupied. The very moment we stepped in the boundaries of that small, lively house, we could feel all the positive vibes that said with every passing second that our bonding would get sturdier. And from together, I mean all three of us. Yes, Mr Colton, since that wasn't our personal house, we couldn't expect it to be all ours. For a few days, we had to share that place with a girl, whom I'd call X. Giving her any name would be an insult to the dignity that the name holds. And as I call her X, I feel sorry for this poor twenty-fourth letter.

Rhea, I could sense, wasn't comfortable, in the beginning, to live with some other girl in the house, wanting both of us to wait for that house to get vacated completely, so that we could live there in privacy, but I refused. I didn't want to let my father see me living with some other girl. He was an honour killer and that scared me the most. Padding of the chosen decision, you see?

And soon our lives came on track, moving swiftly and smoothly. That was what I thought. Though how things happened seemed to be intended, it was all a coincidence. Like I, choosing to stay at that place at the same time X was there for. Like me lying to X about me and Rhea being siblings and she taking it too seriously. Like my insisting Rhea join a hospital in Jagah and X falling in love with me in those moments when I didn't have Rhea beside me in the house.

This came a little too abrupt in the story, no? But that's how it happened to me in real and I didn't get a hint of it. I admit I got a little closer than I was supposed to, but she completely mistook my frankness as something I don't even know. I never understood when her friendship turned into infatuation and infatuation into love. You cannot hold me responsible for not being able to grasp the changes in someone's outlook for me when all of them were happening in a place I had no access to. Her own mind!

To help X's character in your mind, let me be a little evocative. She was one of the most beautiful girls you'd seen in such small towns and for me, she was different than any other girl that I'd come across. She was free from the stereotypes, a little more independent. A girl as dangerous as this breed can get. She hated to be insulted and ignored and I wish I had paid heed to this trait of her a little.

It was yet another day of my and Rhea's life. For X, it wasn't. It was her last day with us as she was leaving for her home town the next day.

She said that she wanted a club party that night and oblivious to her intentions, I spent some quality time in a club, boozing so much that I was hardly in control. But, Mr Colton, no hangover could overtake that of Rhea's love in my life, and when in front of hundreds of people, she proposed her love to me. No prize on guessing my answer.

I took her in a nook to make her understand everything she was supposed to know. She wasn't wrong for she thought Rhea was my sister. I unveiled why I had to lie to her, why I had to leave Jajah, why things went the way they were not supposed to and so that she did not get hurt, I explained to her why everything was an illusion, my mantra to seek pain out of people's life. I thought she would understand, but she didn't.

"You fucking insulted me in front of these people. You damn ignored me in the most suffocating way," she reverted with a shriek.

I strove to explain to her that it wasn't intended, but all in vain. "Done with what you wanted? Now watch me as I teach you what vendetta really means," she said and ran out of the club. She'd halted at the far end for a jiffy, turned back to me and before leaving she said, "Thanks for helping me into your life to destroy you."

I knew she was going to be vindictive, forbidding and what not, but how she decided to destroy me proved that my father wasn't the only man who could make the world go upside down for his ego. I was not in the greatest of my moods the next day. I went for a long drive after dropping Rhea to her clinic. When I returned home in the daytime, the door was open, which meant X was back from her exam, only to shove me into the toughest examination of my life. I saw her, hurting herself, scrapping her own face, cutting her skin and doing everything that was more painful for me to see than to her to feel.

"What are you doing!?"

She watched me as the blood ran down her skin. "You're screwed, man. I hope you get your ass shaved before offering it to the time coming forth."

She laughed the hardest a bleeding girl can.

And this didn't surprise me. I had been through harder experiences of how wrong can people go for honour, ego and a viral called vendetta. I knew what she was planning to do. And I knew it better after reading an article the very morning about how many cases of rape filed in the past three months were fake. More than fifty-three percent! Her words started to relate. *Thanks for letting me in your life to help me destroy you.* She was fucking aware of the fact that if she fooled Rhea into believing all that was cooking in her head, I would have been screwed. Either I had to tell her the truth that I was hiding, or see her leaving me forever.

And when none of them happened, I couldn't believe my luck. I'd asked her to not go home and let X execute her plan. And that was what happened and she, instead of going home, came to the bus stop of the other town, where I was waiting for her.

And, Mr Colton, what so ever is written above is not the truth but what I felt to be true at that point of time. Later I discovered that she'd already gone home and known everything, but was quiet. She pretended to know nothing and I don't know what made her do so. Even if I had the slightest hint about it, instead of feeling triumphant and running from that place to another, I would have explained the truth to her. But instead, this was what happened – we both thought we knew the complete truth and did yet another stupid thing. We went to Kasba, leaving behind that place.

Kasba was the same town Maan had settled in with his father. But, Mr Colton, with a hope of solving everything with time when I went there, I realized someone was following us everywhere. Who? Well, for now just know that he was the real reason behind Preet's murder. Didn't I tell you the theories of investigation teams were just swanky shit?

We met Maan there and as we expected, we couldn't stay at his place for obvious reasons. He, though, arranged a stay for us and I thought I would get to relax a wee in that tranquil place. But I couldn't. Rhea would say that there's something mysterious about the past. It never comes, but never leaves either. That was haunting me.

In the night when Avani was asleep, I went out to breathe some fresh air. I walked on the roads for almost half an hour before I saw a figure emerging from the shadows. I would not have paid heed to him, Mr Colton, had he not come up straight to me, grasped my throat and said, "I'll kill you."

In a dark, deserted street, when someone does that to you, you'll freeze at your place, just like I did. He was in his forties, staring at me with annoyance. Before I could even speak, he said, "That girl you're sleeping with for months... That fucking girl is a murderer, you understand? She murdered my sister and if I was not her so-called maternal uncle, I would have stabbed her to death, just like I got her friend. I would not kill her for she flows the blood of my sister in her, but if anyone tries helping her to live, I wouldn't let anything help him to live. If you doubt my words, you can see what state I sent her friend and her family in, when she tried providing her with a home, with friends, and with freshness. I want her to suffer until she demands death!" He pushed me down.

It was Rhea who was the reason behind Preet's death? Did she actually kill her mother or is this man a psychopath who's blaming an accident on her? But... But it is, oh shit, was it Rhea who was the reason behind the death of Preet! I wondered.

"Just let her rot in solitude. Use her and then fucking throw her. But do not try holding her hand, otherwise you have seen my men in action already, I guess."

Mr Colton, the most frustrating feeling in this world is the realization that the ruthless pain you'd been bearing since so long never belonged to you. With a core so awfully battered that it couldn't even bleed, I moved back into the room. One thing was sure that I was not leaving her alone at any cost, but that man was not someone who could be neglected. He had great power in his hands, and if he could follow us from Jagah to Kasba, just to make sure she doesn't have tranquility in her life, he could do anything to make her life hell. Anything!

I don't understand a thing, Mr Colton. Why is this world more into vendettas than into solutions? I, at least from my personal experiences, believe a forgetful world would make a better place than a vindictive one. Anyway, I wasn't thinking if she'd actually had something hidden from me about the death of her parents and especially that of her mother. I just had to help her out of the situation she wasn't even aware she was in. There was only one way to do that! Flying far off. And if there was only one place I could think of, it was Venice!

I wasn't sure if she'd agree with my decision of flying to Venice. Though I didn't want her to panic by revealing everything if she wasn't going to agree with me to fly here, I'd have had to tell her the truth. But again, she agreed and I thought I'd explain everything once we reached Venice. You know, I had noticed the colour of her face fading the moment she heard that word, maternal uncle, and I realized there was something more than I knew.

We flew to Venice the very next day and went straight to our friends that we'd made when we were here for the first time together. And then happened what I'd never expected. Seeing the magnitude of help we needed from them, his wife stepped back and though he thought he could help us a little, she made him believe they themselves were in no condition to provide us any assistance.

This was a big blow for Rhea and her health deteriorated at seeing herself completely stuck in something that in reality was a solution. But before I could have made her understand that, she lost consciousness. And for the first time in my life, I felt what the horror of finding yourself completely alone in this world of seven billion people feels.

I admitted her in the smallest hospital for I knew I wouldn't be able to bear the charges for her treatment. And that, Andrew Colton, you freakily famous man, listen carefully, that was the worst of the worst decisions I ever took in my life. Or maybe the worst padding up of the worst decision that I had already made. But you need to feel the heat of fire to know it can burn you and only to discover how awfully that decision was going to bounce back onto my face, I needed the amount they were asking for the treatment.

She was in a coma and a horrific thing about a coma is its uncertainty. She could have recovered within hours or not even in years. Though I felt myself shattering seeing her, I had to keep myself standing strong to be able to pay the fees the hospital demanded. And that's how we met, Mr Colton.

I still remember how embarrassingly I pleaded my Venetian friend to help me with something that could make me earn and he asked me about what I could do and I said I'd done nothing other than writing in my life. He was like, dude, that's what my friend needs! When he said that, I wondered if I could really do something great for his friend, and today, when I see you ruling the hearts of millions of fans, I get my answer.

That's how we first met. You'd won a competition for being the first English storyteller of Venice's biggest radio channel. You thought your voice was the best they could get, but not words. And I remember how we had a negotiation about the money you were going to pay me for every story that I wrote for you. And I also remember when I was in my room, on the verge of tears, seeing my life standing at a point so sharp that it was stabbing, when I saw president's tweet on television and how I'd forgotten everything and read that for not less than hundred times. The president of Italy saying that after so long could someone make him cry was big. Do you remember how we quarreled if it was my words or your voice, that made him cry?

"Promise me it'd be a secret that my stories are ghost written. I don't want to lose this fandom."

"What does ghost writing means, by the way?" We'd laughed.

But Mr Colton, in a parallel world, I died every day. With a faint hope in my core that I'd see her opening her eyes, I would go to the hospital every day and return disappointed. For the first two days, I didn't even leave the hospital, but when the management started pressurizing me for the money, I had to be with you for the next two days. And when I went back to the hospital with the money, they said that the M.D. of their hospital, Marshal O' Brien, felt she was not showing any signs of improvement and they had to be paid more for her treatment.

And if you remember I'd told you that I would use pseudonyms for every character, but one. He is that man. He is that fraud. Dr Marshal O' Brien. Mr Colton, when I would go on to describe what a shameless criminal he was, you'd feel so ashamed of being the citizen of the same city he worked in that you would refuse to believe me. But I am a man of my words and I do have the proof. That's why behind this multiple paged letter you'd find something stapled. These stapled things are the statements of the nurses in his hospital, the copy of his fake license, the photographs of the machines he hid in the rooms of patients and the bills that I was given after paying for a treatment that never happened. This is the proof of what I am going to unveil and I feel mortified that I need to prove something like this.

Yes, for the first two days, she was in coma, but she had recovered just after two days. For the next, I wonder how many days, she was just forced into something like a coma and I do not remember the word that nurse had used to explain that to me. You might be wondering which nurse I am talking about, and just be a little patient, because things have just started.

Every time I went to check on Rhea, they would say that she was under critical observation. This happened for almost eight regular days until I went straight to that so-called M.D. and asked him what was wrong. He said he was not going to give me any answers until I paid the full fee. For once, I felt like whacking his face, but instead, I came to you, asked for all the money they wanted me to pay and when you gave me that the next day, I shot myself back to the hospital, throwing the money on their counter.

"What's her room number?"

"She's under critical observation. You can't—"

"Since ten days she's under observation? You sure I am here to talk about a human and not any machine?"

"I am sorry sir, I can't help."

I was determined to not leave the hospital until they let me meet her. But soon she came up to me and asked me to follow her. She took me into a corner and said that she was Mrs Rogan. "Come with me. I'll take you to her room," she said and I followed her. "This one," she pointed towards a room that was between two morgues.

I pushed the door and the room was vacant. I turned my face to her and she gave me a glance as if saying, Yes, that's what the truth is. And, Mr Colton, I would have still controlled myself from not running up to the monitor in the room, unplugging it and throwing it away had I not noticed something that shouldn't have been there. There was a hidden camera on the monitor beside her bed.

"What the hell is this?"

She waited for a pause and then she said what sickened me from inside out. She told me that she'd been working there for two years. That's what he would do. He would pay the nurses to fuck him. She was one of his victims who had slept with him for much-needed money and then got to know his trick. He shot her from one such hidden camera and blackmailed her to be his slave. He was a devil in the body of a handsome prince. The nurse said he made girls fall for him, used them and then got their videos made to sell them to his friend who was developing his own porn portal. He's a sex addict involved in flesh trade. He'd destroyed many lives, one after another. Even her divorce with her husband was because of that piece of stinky shit. She said that she was quiet for a long time, but now she couldn't see more lives being destroyed.

"Where is he? And where is Rhea?"

"He has taken her out. Maybe he'll go to the hotel they do this business in. Hotel Milton."

And yes Mr Colton, that's the name of that hotel. Hotel Milton. The same hotel from where the police caught me when I went there to check if whatever she had said was right. I was a layman. I didn't know how and what to do, so I went directly to the hotel to check on things. To add to my assurance I saw Marshal driving off to the hotel when I reached there.

So I went straight into the hotel and in a low voice said to a man, who was standing in the corner of the hotel. "I am a pimp. Lots of offers. Whom can I meet?"

Mr Colton, that was a huge mistake. You know who he was? The police inspector's PA. I was gone! And as I was busted, the police took me to your friend's house for I had stayed there and my passport was seized. And to make things worse, Rhea was there for a reason completely unknown to me. I was given no chance to even speak.

I am sure I would have ended up losing my life behind bars had you not used all your approach to get me out of there within a month.

The first thing that I did after getting out was contacting Mrs Rogan and knowing where Rhea was and she said they were getting engaged that very day. I asked her why he'd planned an engagement if he only wanted to use her and she said she was confused as well. But she was sure there was something wrong.

And to decipher what that was, I went to their engagement venue. Mr Colton, that was the time life, after so long, gave me a chance to choose again. Either I could have told Rhea everything or I could have told Marshal that I knew everything. The prior was not practically possible. Was she going to believe someone who was a pimp, a rapist and a fucking criminal to her? Obviously not. And if I would have done that, chances were that I'd have been thrown out of the venue. So I took Marshal away for a personal chat.

"Marshal I—" Even before I could have said anything, he took out a revolver from the drawer and pointed it at me.

"I'm aware you know everything. And I also know that if you live, you would tell her everything. But before you die, there's one thing I want you to know. You love her, but so do I. The only difference is that you fucking love her and I love fucking her! Good bye," he said and hooked his finger against the trigger, all set to press it.

I closed my eyes to hear the lullaby of my mother. The wrath of my father. The true meaning of love that Rhea had taught me. The feel of her touch, and for that very second, I swear on these fucking words that I am writing right now, on that very second, I remembered what the colour of her eyes is called.

And when I opened my eyes, he'd already pressed the trigger. Thankfully, there were no bullets in his gun! Before I could run away to protect myself, I saw him jumping onto me. And I killed him! No, that's what the world thinks. In reality, he killed himself. When he jumped on me, I just hitched away and pushed him hard to save myself. But he went on to collide with the wall and his head banged so hard that he was down soon, lying in a pool of blood oozing out of his head. He was dead, Mr Colton, but it was me who died an actual death. I wanted to run to Rhea and tell her I did not do it, but I knew she was not going to believe me, and even if she did, the police were not going to believe me. I was trapped so badly that even you couldn't help me. So I ran away, quitting. Quitting.

That's it. This is my story. I warned you it would make no sense and, Mr Colton, it doesn't. I ended up being a man who strove a little too hard to fix the broken pieces. And when I forced the broken pieces of my life to stick back, they ended up slashing my life. I told you, unspoken words often add up to create the darkest stories and all those words that should have been shared between us, that were left unspoken, are adding now and revealing the ruthless story of my worthless life.

Thank you for your time, Mr Colton, to read the story of my life. I wish it was beautiful, but somewhere I failed. As I write these words, I don't know what my future is ahead, but, Mr Colton, I must confess I am tired. I am just tired of me. I am tired of hurting her. I am tired of seeing my pathetic face in the mirror.

Mr Colton, my upbringing was not the best. The ruthless world had already taken my mother, I witnessed abuses of solitude, I felt homesickness even after being at home. Though I don't mean to brag about myself, I feel I am a champion who fought hard to keep the human within himself alive, but today, Mr Colton, today, once more, I lost.

I am tired of remembering how feeling good feels like. I never wanted to be the person I am right now, but now, I don't want to be the person I was, as well. You know why? Because I am tired, Mr Colton, I am tired. As I look at my life, I feel as if I am tired of each and every possible thing in this world, apart from one. You know what? To think about her.

I am not sure about it, but if one day she gets to know about this reality, she would isolate herself into all those feelings I tolerated to save her from. Guilt! And I know she'd wait for me to come and collect the pieces of her broken heart to make it beat for me again, but I won't come. And this time, not because I am too tired, but because this life is a myth and every breath of ours is an illusion. And once the illusion ends, you step into reality so engrossing that you're stuck there forever. And Mr Colton, it's possible to return to reality from an illusion, but not into an illusion from reality. Isn't it? And I am going to step in that reality, leaving this illusion – that people call life – behind.

I wonder if we would meet like two rivers, melding and moulding into each other. Because, Mr Colton, I swear in that moment, when I'd run to her and she to me, it would be the last time we'll reunite, because we would never be apart again.

I don't want to die, Mr Colton, somebody please help me out of this. But wait, let it be. I am tired of this illusion.

I—

"Stop it!" An army of police climbs up on the stage before he can finish it. A police officer moves to him with three gunmen besides him and says, "You're under arrest, Mr Andrew Colton. Kindly cooperate."

Andrew Colton smiles.

"Ayaan Anand is dead," Andrew Colton said, gnashing his teeth. "And I have been saying this to you since four days."

"You haven't done any work of Sherlock, Mr Colton." The superintendent of police took his spectacles off and sat on the chair opposite Colton's. "It's clearly written at the bottom of the letter which, thankfully, you couldn't read."

The SP stretched out his hand at his junior police officer and he provided him with the letter cum booklet that Andrew Colton was reading from. After flipping through a few pages, he put his spectacles on and said, "Here it is. It's written in pretty good handwriting that he is committing suicide."

"That's what my point is. That's what I have been telling you since four days and still, I am getting called here every day for hours."

"Dear storyteller, he has written he's committing suicide but what's following it is that he's done it at a place that, he says, you know pretty well."

"That's what he thought. I repeat, I do not know what he was thinking while writing that. Are you even understanding what I am trying to say?"

"Calm down. We know you're quite troubled after your friend's death, but this is something more than your stories and your fans." He stands up and moves around his chair. "It is about real life murders and deaths, and if you ask me why am I calling you here every day, it's because of the orders from not only our seniors, but also from the Indian police. It's because you know many things associated with Mr Marshal's murder and that girl's murder in India."

"Haven't I already told you I know nothing?"

"You did. But how do we believe that? How do we believe you don't know that girl Rhea, if I go as per her pseudonym and Avani if I go by her real name that we got to know from that fraud hospital's staff?"

"Because his letter was as shocking for me as it was for you. We never talked too much apart from our work."

"That's not the proof, Mr Colton. This matter has turned more serious than it should have had. The international media has been talking about it. You should have brought this cluster of papers to us before going out there and being a hero."

Andrew Colton looks at the SP with engaging eyes and says, "That was up to me to decide. If you're done with your work, I think I should leave."

As he stands up to walk past the exit door of the chamber, a man enters in with a laptop in his hand and says, "Sir, we've found something in his emails."

Andrew Colton watched him and looked at the S.P. with surprise. "You have been looking into my e-mails? That's hacking!"

"It's police investigation," he said and took the laptop in his hands. "What did you find?"

Andrew Colton walked near the SP to have a sneak peek.

"This!" The man said and clicked on an e-mail from avanibibliophile@ymail.com

❖

Hello Mr Andrew Colton,

To begin with a clumsy note, I never expected you to read this but I am so happy you're doing it. Not for me, but for you. Your reading it or not is not putting any difference to my lifeless life, but it might end up having an impact on yours, I guess.

You must be wondering the authenticity of this claim and more than that would you wonder that of the sender's. Mine! You'd ask who the hell I am and I'd say you know me pretty well, Mr Colton. I am a character of your last story. Rhea! Avani, in real life.

I'm not sure if you've already read such emails where fake accounts claimed themselves to be Rhea, to get your attention, but as I said it's you not me who'd be affected by not believing it. I wonder how I am typing this email at a stage where my senses should have gone numb from this colossal pain. Is it because those stories still inspire me, or because finally, it's my time to return what all that you gave me?

Don't take what's coming forth as the justification of my crime. I am just gonna speak my heart out before it ceases to exist. Ayaan, you know, was knitting my life. You think it's getting complicated, but it's slowly developing you into what you can be. Probably that's what he came into my life for. He taught me all the things I never knew existed and when I learned that life is nothing but a mere illusion, he left as if he himself was an illusion who had come to show me the reality.

There were two things that he would tell me. The first one being that there are two worlds that exist. One, that we live in, consisting of all the things that we believe are true, and the other one's home to all those things that are hidden from us, but is the truth. He would warn me, Mr Colton, to never mistake my knowledge of things with the merging of both the worlds. He would tell me that no matter how sure we are, that world still exists behind our back, larger than the one we're living in.

But that's what I ended up doing. I thought all that I knew was how things were and that's when I merged both the worlds so hard that both of them shattered. And today when I see my world shattered, it reminds me of the second thing he would always say. Every breath is an illusion.

He was so right, Mr Colton, and I don't think it can ever get so painful realizing that your love was right and you were not. This thing should always make someone happy, but I am not. Thanks for opening my eyes because today when I look back into his life and into my life and then into our life, I realize that every breath we were taking together was mere illusion. Maybe he was thinking of me to be someone who had some dark past with her mother, but that was not the truth. My maternal uncle was such a brother who could die for his sister and when he saw his sister dying because of me, he lost his mental balance. He wanted vendetta. I thought it was for a few months before he would realize it wasn't my fault, but I never knew it would turn my life upside down.

And I, oh, I was so delusional that I think I need not explain. I was in an illusion that he was wrong and he was in an illusion that things would get better. It hurts, and it hurts so hard!

Thank you for letting me know where I'll find him. In reality. At least I would waste no more time searching for him in this illusion. Before I go to meet him again and reunite for the last time, I think I should let you know that your voice is better than one's ears can bear.

Okay, Mr Colton, tada! It's my time to head back to that path. The path which introduced us will connect us once again. I am going towards it!

Much Love.

"The path which introduced us will connect us once again?" The SP squints at Andrew Colton and asks, "What does that mean?" Andrew Colton shrugs.

"Figure out the sender's address quickly." The other man nods and takes the laptop with him to his cabin.

"What did she mean?" Andrew Colton mumbled to himself.

"It's from India, sir," he says. "A town called Jagah."

"Make a call to the police headquarters of Jagah," the SP ordered. The officer nods, searching for the number on the internet and telephones there, keeping it on loudspeaker.

After a long wait, a voice from the other end spoke, "Jagah Police station."

"Hello. I am superintendent of police calling from Venice, Italy. May I know whom am I talking to?"

"Regards, sir. I am Jaydev Thakur. Police Inspector, Jagah. How may I help you?"

"Mr Thakur, I need some information about an Indian girl who just flew back there from Venice, if you could."

"Eh, please hold the line sir," he said and they heard him asking his junior the name of a girl whose passport was seized from the venue he was talking about. "Are you there, sir?"

"Yes, Mr Thakur."

"Was her name Avani?" He shocked them.

"Oh yes, Mr Thakur."

"The details that we have about her are that she was found dead at Jagah Railway Station yesterday. She jumped under train number 61414 at 1:10 p.m. IST. Is that what you want to know?" No response from other end.

"The path which introduced us wo—" Andrew Colton stopped midway, realizing what Avani meant.

The laptop screen was open, though only dusk spread over it. A red bulb fought vainly to shine brighter than the sunlight coming from the window. The air reeked of sweat and there were mice running all around on the bed, table, window frame, chair and almost everywhere. There was a cluster of papers under which was the rental bill for the laptop.

A pair of mice ran swiftly on the table, and one of them struck a photo frame. A sharp sound of breaking glass echoed in the room and her eyes opened in deep horror.

Woah!

She stared around. A suffocating room. A wall clock said it was 12:30. A laptop. Papers. Oh fuck, I was dreaming! She realized it was all a dream. She tried to remember and failed. Her eyes fell on the cluster of papers on her table and she realized all of what should have been a dream was reality.

Those papers were the letters that Ayaan had written to Andrew Colton. It had leaked through the sources of media and as she read it again, she felt she was doing it for almost the millionth time.

I quit, Mr Colton. I knew nothing's still lost. I knew even now I can hold her hand and she mine and we could start it all over again. But I am tired, Mr Colton. I am so tired to even give it a try. I quit. I am taking a step that I never thought belonged to me, but then life's called unpredictable. I would die. A suicide or a murder, your choice of words. You know where I'd do that. So if ever she comes running to you with tears in her eyes, wanting you to take her to the place I last breathed, do bring her here. She would feel better!

She cries.

Everything apart from Andrew Colton in the police headquarters hearing of Avani's death was the truth. And her death, a dream. Fuck you with a sharply pointed shaft, life!

She brings the laptop screen to life and there it is! The e-mail that she'd written for Andrew Colton, but before she could send it, she dozed off. She watches the time and it's 12:45. The path which introduced us would connect us once again. She's left with just twenty-five minutes. But thankfully, the hotel room she has checked in for a night is very close to Jagah Railway Station.

Deep breaths. Eyes closed. A couple of gulps. And there she goes. Up to you, Mr Colton. Here I go! She thinks to herself and clicks the send button.

She reaches down and jumps into a rickshaw which drops her to the railway station in ten minutes. There are millions of options for her to kill herself without having to do so much, but no; she had no choice over her birth, but she wants it on her death. She wants to get connected to him on the same path they were introduced on.

The same place. Tranquility just like before. The same zeal in people. Oh, it all feels like the first time. Somebody fly her back to those moments. Alas, nobody can do that for her apart from that one thing that she has come here for. Death!

"Train number 61414 will arrive at platform number one at the scheduled time." The same platform? This fucking destiny.

With every passing second, her heart beats faster. She wants to die. She has to die. She will die. Death had been calling her since forever and had she accepted it back then, she wouldn't have to feel it. The more she tried running away from agony, the more it bashed her. She doesn't have any courage left in her. And as the time inches closer, she feels she would die of a heart attack before the arrival of the train. Death doesn't come that easy, after all. A couple of minutes are left and she is fighting her own demons.

Stop! What are you doing? This is not what Ayaan wanted you to be.

Do not listen to her. What has life given you anyway? Pain, pain, and pain?

You can't forget the cure of pain is in pain itself. Wasn't that the first thing that Ayaan had taught you?

Ayaan is dead. His teachings didn't even work when he was alive.

If you'll take that step, it would be the biggest cheating you'd do. You'd kill the thing he died for, and more than that, you'd kill the existence of his life with you. Until the last moment he taught you how to overcome pain, and if today you surrender to pain, mistaking this illusion as reality, his life will lose existence.

Don't listen to her.

Don't listen to her.

Get lost.

You get lost.

"Where are you running to?" She feels a hand on her shoulder in union with the honking of the approaching train and she jumps away in terror, almost falling on the track.

Avani turns back and as her eyes meet his, her heart almost explodes. The blood's not running in her veins anymore and she doesn't even know she is supposed to breathe, let alone jump under the train that's already crossing her now.

"Ayaan!" She screeches, her eyes so wide open that they hurt. "You! Here!"

She tries to pinch herself to check if it's not a dream, yet again, and her hands are quivering so bad that she can't even do that. She's not dreaming, she knows. Ayaan the fucking Anand is right in front of her eyes, just like the first time.

"Woah! That reaction's weird." He smiles as if everything's normal.

"You... you, you're still alive?"

"Alive?" He squints. That word confuses him for a while before he understands the thing. "Oh, don't tell me you heard that Andrew Colton story!"

"You said you were dying." She weeps.

Ayaan smiles, moving closer to her, and embraces her in his arms. This is heaven! She is now ready to die.

"I didn't even know that you knew Andrew Colton," he says and looks directly into her eyes. He's so mystical. "What all he said was true, but that doesn't mean I had to do all that I wrote. Does that?"

She shakes her head, crying like a little baby.

"But thankfully, he's eased my things out. Now I can explain you everything in a better way." Ayaan takes her a little away from the edge of the track. "I was so frustrated seeing myself stuck in that trap that I had to die or else the Venetian police would have killed me. I had my own choices when it came to death. But death is something that losers opt for. Though, that doesn't mean I wasn't a loser."

She shakes her head again, even after knowing she should nod.

"So, I had my mind set. If they were going to catch me at the airport, I was going to surrender, and if I was going to escape Venice before my passport could be seized again, I was going to die here under the same train, in which you came for the first time. I know you're wondering how my mind could have worked so senselessly deep!? Are you?"

She nods. She's not even listening to what he's saying. She's just lost. The train screams as it passes behind her, at its full speed, though still slower than her heartbeats.

"But when I reached here, I called Joe to know if everything was fine in Venice. It took him so long to believe I was alive but when he was sure, he informed me that he'd booked your tickets for Sheher. And I was actually shocked, you know. But then I thought if you were coming to Sheher, you were surely coming here. And see how right I was.

The baby nod comes again.

"So I went to the airport to check on your flight, but I didn't see you until you boarded a cab to leave. I followed you until you checked into a hotel. I thought you didn't know the truth, so I didn't ask the hotel to call you. Of course, I didn't want any drama in public. I waited until the morning and finally when I saw you, you were gone in a rickshaw. I followed you till here. I thought you were leaving Jagah, so ripping apart all my fears of facing your wrath in public, I approached you. Thankfully you knew everything already. Eh… so yeah, here I am, finally, in front of you. Alive."

She's quiet, looking into his eyes.

"Say something?"

"I love you Ayaan!" Her voice quivered.

"Haha! Come, let's go!"

"Where? And what if the cops catch you now?"

"I'm very cautious though, but even if something goes wrong, my dad will look after it."

"Your dad?" She asks shocked.

"Oh, I forgot! You know, when I came back, I went home to see my mother's photograph for the last time. I thought he was going to hit me. But you know Avani," Ayaan almost jumps as he says that, "The moment I confronted him, he walked up to me and hugged me like anything. After almost a decade. And I'd still have been oblivious about it had Kaka not told me that even he had heard Andrew Colton's last story." He chuckles.

"Ayaan."

"Yes?"

"You proved again, that no matter how sure we are, that world is always bigger than this one." She grinned. He gave her a warm smile.

Avani's emotions erupted. "I can't believe it's really happening. I mean, I was supposed to be dead by now. Such a change over with such a pace. Oh fuck, things can't be so perfect. I can't believe it."

"What if it's an illusion and—"

"Fuck off, Ayaan."

'No, really. I mean the second world still exists and–'

'Fuck. Off. Ayaan.'

"By the way, dad wants me to marry you this month itself."

"Really?"

"Fuck off, Avani."

Epilogue

2 years later

Hi,

I think this e-mail surprises you but certainly you're not the only one who can surprise people by your instant e-mails. It's been long, so damn long and I hope many things would have changed. I am writing this to you, because right now, I am in a city I don't think I will again be in. So, even if you try finding my location out, it wouldn't help you.

I am not sure if I sound rude, Ayaan, but please don't mistake it with any sort of anger in me. I don't blame Avani or you for the death of my sister and I know that you know that! It's just that every time I think of you and her, I fly back into the time that never gives me good memories. But I still love you and will keep doing that. Until the end of forever.

Ayaan, whenever I sit and think about our lives, I realize we all were the people of pain. If ever someone would sum up our stories in few words, it would turn out to be a journey of shattered lives, a tale that would show what happens when wrecked lives meet, fuse and fight against the agony. There was pain in your life. In Avani's life. In my life. In my father's life. And in the united life of us all.

When I relive those memories, I realize there is more pain in fighting the pain than in pain itself. But it would bend one day, no matter how strong is it. That is what has happened in our lives. Avani never accepted her defeat, you never knelt down to it and even I never allowed it to rule me, and after so long, I see our lives happy. But still, there was someone who couldn't fight against the pain for long.

You know Ayaan, after you left for Venice, within a week, dad died. His liver had rotted so bad that he couldn't be healed. I was left alone. So alone. But I never let the pain rule me and as a consequence, I am smiling right now.

I giggle as I tell you that I am married to someone who helped me with this battle like Avani was with you. The strangest part about it is that you and Avani, both know my wife, but hey, stop guessing because even after millions of efforts, you would never get the name right. Neither expect me to tell anything about her. Let her be a known stranger in your lives.

We're blessed with a daughter. She's so beautiful. She speaks three words as of now. Pa, Ma and ruri (that has no meaning, though.) You know what we call her? We call her Luv. And she's as beautiful as Luv was.

Ayaan, it's worthless to tell you this, as you already know everything, but sometimes life takes such sharp turns that your vision for life-left-behind blocks. That's what my life has done. It has provided me with more than it snatched from me and there's one thing that's still the same. A thing called hope. I believe if hope's gone, your life becomes a true example of worthlessness.

With every morning that I wake up, I give birth to a new hope in me. I have a hope that someday when I walk on my roads, I'd find a woman coming to me from the far end. I'd keep looking her and she'd do the same until one of us would realize we're akin. I imagine her running towards me, telling me how she was abducted and how her life was hell without me. I would cry in her arms and she'd wipe my tears off, and after ages,

I would realize what having a mother feels like. I hope one day I would find her, lost in this world, and one day the world of my soreness would get lost forever.

But, Ayaan, I have a hope of a real thing as well. You know what? A hope that when my life would be a complete mess and I'd be running around, finding solutions, I would bang into you and it would all happen out of luck. You'd expect me to talk about all the years we couldn't be a part of each others' lives, and instead I would frown, cry and tell you how bad the world has been screwing me. You'd nod, wink and then show me all the solutions, like you always did. And I'd get amazed seeing you being a wizard when it comes to perception towards troubles. I would ask you why, why do you never fall short of solutions to all the problems in this world, and you'd smile, pat my shoulder, look into my eyes and say, because every breath is an illusion!